Big Sky

BIG SKY

KITTY THOMAS

Burlesque Press

Big Sky
© 2012 by Kitty Thomas

Printed in the United States of America

ISBN-13 978-1-938639-05-0

Wholesale orders can be placed through Ingram.

Published by Burlesque Press

Contact: burlesquepress@gmail.com

For M.

Acknowledgments

Thank you to the following people for their help and contributions in the making of *Big Sky*

Robin Ludwig for cover art.

Natasha for copyedits and developmental edits.

Emma, Kimberly, Stephannie, Michelle, and Claudia for beta reading.

Stephannie for her ranch expertise.

M for his love and support.

Disclaimer

This is a work of fiction, and the author does not endorse or condone any behavior done to another human being without their consent.

Warning: This book is meant for a mature audience and contains:

One

Veronica rolled over to the unimpressive view outside her window: another building far too close to her own. On the mornings when she woke abruptly, it felt as if the building might collide with hers, as if the concrete sidewalks and asphalt roads were a rumbling sea that would toss the buildings to and fro, annihilating anyone in its path.

She stumbled to the kitchen and poured a cup of burnt coffee then went back to the window in an attempt to glimpse the tiny bit of sky she could see from just the right angle. The morning was dreary and overcast—one of those days where the sky would share its contempt for the world by being bleak but unproductive. It would be a day without sun or rain, just an unending and depressing blob of gray.

It was possible the angst was less from the weather and more from the pile of bills on the kitchen counter. Veronica Cason was a Big Deal ad executive. Yes, that's in capital letters, thank you. As a Big Deal she should be in a penthouse apartment overlooking Central Park.

But Veronica had always lived outside her means. Extravagantly outside them. It didn't matter how much those means were, she'd never seen a credit card she couldn't max out, and she had a rainbow of them that fluttered out of her wallet in a fan of spending power.

She'd started in a penthouse, and when her credit bills had swelled to a wave that would otherwise swallow her, she'd downshifted into a tiny apartment with no sky. And this was where she'd stayed for the past five years while she'd tried to curb her overspending without success. After all, it took more work and more money to make an ugly apartment habitable. These were justifiable expenditures. A raise could be on the horizon, then perhaps she could finally dig out of the collection call nightmare.

The interest rates on some of the cards were so criminal that if she only paid the minimum, she'd continue to owe more than she started out with—her debt climbing higher with each passing year. She could consolidate, but that was most of her paycheck, leaving her on Ramen noodles, which she didn't need. Though her finances were a wreck, she did mange self control in her diet. After all, she thought it was pointless to buy stylish clothes in the big girl sizes. When she felt the urge for ice cream, she just bought another dress and pair of Manolo Blahniks. Fat or destitute were the only options her mind would consider, and cardboard box felt more encouraging than size fourteen.

A piece of paper glared from the pile, a bright orange rectangle, a corner of which peeked out from the sea of perfunctory white and light blue. It was an eviction notice from her landlord. Mr. Tuttle had become clever—or so he thought—with his increasingly bright warning notices: pink to neon green, to yellow, to finally orange when he'd dropped the hammer and given her thirty days to get out. That had been twenty-seven days ago.

But it was fine. She had a plan. She'd just use her next paycheck to secure another crappy apartment. She'd get on eBay and start selling off all the ridiculous things she'd acquired. The seriousness of the situation had finally struck home. Her denial had run out only moments before her lease. She had nobody but herself, and she'd systematically sabotaged her security. She could have determined why, but a shrink was a luxury she couldn't afford right now—even with a co-pay.

Her father had left when she was six, and her mother had moved to Rome without a forwarding address. She couldn't ask friends for help. Anyone who could be defined loosely as a friend, she worked with, and she couldn't let them know where she lived now—let alone the fact that she was about to be homeless on a six-figure salary. It was too ludicrous and humiliating. Going back to bed and waiting for the building next door to collide and crush her was beginning to sound like an appealing option.

Veronica put the cup on the counter. Screw this shit. She was going out for breakfast.

The diner across the street from Brampton and Simmons Advertising Agency had an inexpensive breakfast that Veronica wouldn't feel as guilty about putting on her credit card. She reached out for the door, but a large, tanned hand—no tiny sliver of sky for him—got there first.

"Let me get that for you, ma'am."

Veronica looked up, annoyed to see what looked like the Marlboro man, complete with a cowboy hat, holding the door for her.

"Do you live in a corn field? I can open my own damned doors." Had it been a business man in a suit, and had she been carrying something big and heavy, she wouldn't have protested, but they were far from *Little House on the Prairie*, and she wasn't too feeble to open a door.

He raised an eyebrow. Not amused. Not angry. Just . . . observant. Creepy. He was attractive in a sun-worn way, but the assessing look he gave her made her want to crawl under a table and hide. Or maybe that was just her life.

She glared at him and finally he took a step back, his hands raised in the air as if he were an outlaw caught without his gun. She rolled her eyes and went inside.

It was a seat-yourself sort of place, so Veronica took a spot by the window. But there was no view.. The monolithic buildings rose out of the ground like oppressive guardians, with only a small bit of gray sky visible between her office building and the building next door.

She ordered scrambled eggs and hot tea and tried not to stare at the Marlboro man who had seated himself a few booths down where he could watch her.

The act unnerved her. She felt stalked, but she'd pulled out the feminist annoyance at not being treated like an equal who could open her own doors. Scurrying like a mouse to a corner booth out of his line of sight would seem to make light of her independence. Instead, she pulled out her smart phone to check her email.

Five minutes later, the bell over the door dinged, and in walked Sandy Mitchell. At best, the woman was a frenemy. They worked together—if one could call their constant battlefield behavior working *together*.

"Ronnie!" She smiled and waved with the fake bright-ness that was her calling card. Her modus operandi was to kill with kindness. She looked smart in an aquamarine suit that brought out her impossibly blue-green eyes. Without invitation, she sat across from Veronica and flipped her blonde hair. At least she was mostly blocking the Marlboro man now. Or at least she was serving as a distraction—

something else to look at besides tanned, muscular arms, tight jeans, and cowboy boots.

"Just coffee for me, thanks," she told the waitress when she arrived with the eggs and tea.

Sandy pulled out a small, pink laptop when they were alone again. "Did you come up with a slogan for the Waterson account?"

No, the stress of being evicted put a damper on my creative skills.

"Several," Veronica lied, not willing to let Sandy see the cards she didn't have to play.

"Great! Can I see them?"

Nice try.

"Did you come up with any?" Veronica deflected.

"Only five, but I'm not sure they'll like any of them."

Like hell she wasn't sure. Sandy liked to play the defenseless kitten routine, which every man in the office ate up like slow-roasted pulled pork at a BBQ stand. If Mr. Marlboro had opened the door for her, she would have batted her eyelashes, melted into girl-goo, and made a date with him for after work. They'd be fucking by seven-thirty on the dot. She'd no doubt pull the *I never do this with strangers* routine by eight. He'd be out the door by nine, in plenty of time for her beauty sleep so she could be perfect again by morning. Sandy Mitchell? *Not* a feminist.

Veronica glanced over to Mr. Marlboro's table. He'd ordered enough food for a small army. It might take him an hour to get through the pancakes, sausage, biscuits, eggs, bacon, and milk surrounding him. It was a heart attack waiting to happen, but he was in such good shape he could probably fend it off with brute strength. She forced herself to look away before she could determine if he had a milk mustache.

Sandy dropped her voice an octave and leaned forward in the less-than-subtle way she did. "Did you see the hot guy over there?"

Of course Sandy would zero in on any eligible-for-copulating male within a mile radius. Veronica feigned confusion.

"You know . . . the cowboy." She whispered the word *cowboy*. "He could ride me any day."

Veronica choked a little on her eggs. She took a sip of tea and composed herself. "Oh, the Neanderthal who thinks women are too frail to open doors? Yeah, he's a peach."

Sandy rolled her eyes and flipped her hair again, turning briefly to give him an obvious once-over and no doubt a come-hither smile, but Marlboro Man's eyes were on Veronica, still cataloging and assessing. He was probably a serial killer.

"Why do you hate men so much?" Sandy hissed when she turned back around.

"I don't *hate* men. I just expect to be treated like a human being and not some fragile doll. I'm not some pet or lesser being. Would he have opened the door for another man?"

She shrugged. "Who cares? He's pretty. If you didn't overanalyze the wrong things, you could have a boyfriend by now."

"Oh right. Because landing a man is one of the life goals of every female. It was in the woman manual I was sent at puberty."

"It is unless you're a lesbian. *Are* you a lesbian?" Sandy pulled her jacket closed to hide the girls a little, as if Veronica would leap across the table and dive head first into her cleavage.

"No. I'm not a lesbian. When I find an enlightened man who respects me as an equal, I'll think about letting one into my life. I have a vibrator for God's sake."

The waitress came back with Sandy's coffee and a check for Veronica.

"Oh, please. No straight woman wants equality in the bedroom. They want a dominant alpha male to throw them down and growl and grunt a little."

"Classy. And could you please keep your voice down?"

But the Marlboro man had heard. There was that eyebrow again. Veronica stared at the small bit of eggs left on her plate, wondering if he was aware of the warm flush that had come to her cheeks at Sandy's description. What one fantasized about and what one was willing to actually do could be continents apart. Everybody knew that, with the exception of Sandy Mitchell.

The morning meeting was a disaster—for everyone but Sandy, who would most likely receive Veronica's office and a raise after this.

"Ms. Cason, you've been *off* for months now. You weren't prepared for the meeting. I was going to let you take the lead on the Waterson account, but you gave me nothing."

Normally Joe called her Ronnie like everybody else. He only pulled out the formal Ms. Cason when he was disappointed with her. Something in his demeanor grated on every indignant cell in her body—like he was being condescending because she was a woman, and he'd been proven right on her incompetence.

"I'm sorry. All right? I've got some personal stuff going on." The quasi-apology took all her willpower to muster.

"What personal stuff?"

If she told Joe her financial situation, he might feel some pity and help her out, but either way it would be all over the office by noon.

"Never mind."

"I'm going to have to let you go, Ronnie." Now it was the more personal form of address, the name to soften the blow and make him sound like a good guy who was simply left with no other alternatives.

If it had been Sandy, she would have collapsed into tears and begged. She would have sandwiched some flirting in there somewhere, and she would have walked out with a better office. But Veronica couldn't bring herself to play the helpless girl card. It offended everything inside her. She turned and headed for her office.

Her boss's voice stopped her. "Don't you have anything to say?"

"What should I say, Joe? I already said I was sorry. I'm not delving into my personal life with you. I'm not going to grovel or cry or scream at you like some petulant child. You've made your decision. I'm going to pack my desk if you don't mind."

"Give me anything, Ronnie. Any indication that things will get better, here. You're brilliant when you want to be, but you isolate yourself. I can't help you if you don't let me."

"I didn't ask for help. Are you firing me or not?"

"You've left me no choice."

"What about unemployment? Are you going to put it down that I was laid off or fired?"

"You know Human Resources won't let me say you were laid off. They watch that stuff more closely now."

"Fine."

Thirty minutes later, she was sitting on the marble slab that encircled the fountain in front of Brampton and Simmons. With her back to the building and her box of things in her hands—a fake plant, a book, and a handful of nice fountain pens—it was finally safe to cry. Since the sky had betrayed her again, opening to allow rain to pour down, she could do it with a small amount of privacy even in public.

She was so lost in her own misery that she didn't realize she wasn't alone until the dark brown cowboy boots were only a few inches away from her.

She scooted away. "What do you want?"

"Lose your job?"

"Well, look at the box and the pathetic girl crying in the rain. Figure it out, genius."

"You're rude."

"Another brilliant observation," she said. "You'll make it great in the big city."

The rain came down harder. The cowboy stood tall and steady in the downpour as if he were part of the elements and silly things like weather couldn't touch him.

"Let me buy you a cup of coffee."

Had he been lurking and waiting for her? "Why? Do you get off on being yelled at?" Just what she needed. One of *those* freaks.

In answer, he offered a hand to help her stand. It was a public place. And anyway, if he killed her, that might be a step up from the current situation. She had no idea what she was going to do. She'd considered bankruptcy—assuming she could afford the fees to file. But that was out now. It would make it that much harder to find another job, if anybody in the industry even wanted her now. She'd hopped from job to job over the past few years burning bridges with abandon. There might not be any left for her to walk across.

Veronica threw her box of things in the trash on the way to the diner. None of it had sentimental value, and it was all ruined anyway. She tried not to wince or scream at him as he led her inside, his hand resting at the small of her back like he was calling dibs on her and wanted to warn away all other males.

There were no other males in the diner—just the cook, whose name she didn't know.

A familiar waitress came out and led them to a booth. "Oh sweetie, you look like a drowned sewer rat."

"Thanks," Veronica said.

"Let me get you a towel to dry off."

Marlboro man looked somewhat drenched himself, but she didn't offer him a towel, nor did he seem to care for one. It was possible Veronica was a lot more pathetic-looking than she thought.

"I'm Luke," he said, after he'd ordered them some coffee and Veronica was seated in the booth with a towel wrapped around her.

There was a long pause where she couldn't think what to say. He probably wasn't going to kill her in the middle of the diner.

"Ronnie, is it? Is that short for something?" he finally asked. He must have heard Sandy say her name that morning.

"V-Veronica." It was the chill from the rain that had made her stutter. Or that was the story she was going with. She couldn't bring herself to be nasty to him again after he'd bought her a cup of coffee. This was the kind of thinking that got women lured into the middle of nowhere and killed.

"The reason I brought you in for coffee is that I have a ranch in Vermont. I could always use another hand out there."

She looked up, startled. He really *did* plan to lure her to the middle of nowhere. With the way he'd watched her earlier that morning with Sandy, there was no way in hell. "I'm sorry, what?"

"It's not advertising with a slick office, but it comes with room and board."

Images of being kept prisoner by him in some barn filled her head. She tried not to be aroused by those images. Now wasn't the time for those thoughts. It wouldn't play out like her fantasies. He was just so attractive, it was hard not to think those thoughts.

"I'll be fine. I'm really more of a city girl."

"I make you uncomfortable."

She made a face. "Don't be ridiculous."

Veronica jumped when he went for his wallet, and he arched a brow. That eyebrow had a mind and life of its own.

He unfolded the smooth leather and slid an ivory business card across the table. The font was Palatino Linotype—classy, and not at all what she'd expect from a Rancher. She wondered if he'd picked it himself or if someone named Kimberly or Tiffany had suggested it. The ink was in burnt umber. There was a crude image—almost like a stencil—of a G with steer horns coming out of it—also in the brown ink. In the middle of the ivory rectangle were the words: *Granger Ranch, Luke Granger, owner.* An address and phone number were in the lower left, along with a website.

For the briefest moment, Veronica pretended she'd take his offer and that he wasn't potentially dangerous. The business card painted a nice, peaceful scene far from the stress of the city.

"The guys convinced me to take a much-needed vacation, so I'll be here til the end of next week. You can call me if you change your mind. That number is my cell. I always have it on me."

"I don't think I will." She slid the card back in his direction.

He shrugged. "Suit yourself. Keep the card. I got a bulk discount." He laid some money on the table and walked out of the diner.

The waitress sat two cups of coffee down on the table. "Is he coming back?"

"Probably not," Veronica said, unsure if she was relieved or disappointed.

"Shame. He's a fine looking cowboy. He could ride me any day."

It seemed to be the sentiment of the day.

Veronica sat at the kitchen table with her pile of bills, credit cards, and a bowl of Ramen noodles, keenly aware of how close to nothing she was. Between the bad economy and her colorful job history, her industry as a whole seemed to have decided they were no longer buying what she was selling. Even crappy jobs outside her industry were in short supply these days. Moving to a new city required money she didn't have, so that was out.

Being confronted with the reality of her finances and job prospects in such short order was bracing to say the least.

Luke's business card sat to the side. It reminded her of a famous short story: "The Lady or the Tiger" by Frank Stockton. The only thing she remembered of the story was that a man was presented with two doors. Behind one of them was a beautiful woman who presumably he would take as his wife. Behind the other was a tiger that would maul him to death.

The Rancher's offer felt like that kind of choice. She could choose to stay in the city and try to put her life back together. She could end up pulling it together and having a happy ending, or as a prostitute in an alleyway strung out on heroin. Similarly, if she went with Luke, she could end up safe and happy or in a hole in the ground. It was impossible to know which choice would result in her death, but she felt certain one of them would.

Her credit cards were laid out in a row, ready to be put in the appropriate pile: maxed out or usable. Given her current predicament, all maxed cards would have to be cut up, the others she'd have to live on sparingly, along with her last paycheck, until she could work something else out. She stacked her most current credit card statements in the order the cards were in.

"Maxed out, maxed out, maxed out, maxed out, usable, maxed out, maxed out, usable, usable, Victoria's Secret . . . " Victoria's Secret wasn't maxed, but it had to go in the maxed pile. A card to a lingerie store couldn't feed her—or actually it could, but she wasn't about to go down that road. "maxed out, maxed out, maxed out." The rest were department store cards which suffered the same unfortunate drawback of Victoria's Secret.

Even with her income, it shouldn't have been possible for her to acquire so many credit cards. And yet here she was: five Visas, four Mastercards, one Discover card, three American Express cards, and all the rest. Three cards were still usable. One Mastercard and two Visas. Each card had less than two hundred dollars available. She had one paycheck coming in two days and a final check in two weeks. A little under five thousand dollars to her name after taxes, including credit cards. Even if they weren't maxed, she'd have to get rid of the American Express. The annual fees were too much on top of everything else.

Veronica cut up the bad cards, but rationalized keeping the store cards. After all, if she had no apartment, there was only so much she could carry with her. People needed clothes. She felt like a fugitive. She wouldn't be able to get an apartment even as nice as the one she was in without proof of current employment. And if she dropped to the next level down, she might as well be the heroin-addicted whore in the alley.

Two

A week and a half later found her in a deserted park looking like a bag lady. She'd had to be forcibly removed from her apartment. She'd been to all the employment agencies, but the only things available—she was overqualified for. What did that even mean? If you could do more, couldn't you just as easily do less and take the pay cut?

She'd ended up taking only a couple of bags of personal belongings; paying for storage would only get her in a soup kitchen line sooner. She'd thought about selling her stuff on eBay, but the logistics of running an online store from a cheap hotel room while she was running out of money stopped her. She'd be robbed blind if she brought most of that stuff to where she was currently staying, anyway.

It was only a matter of time before the money ran out, and she didn't want to think about what would happen then.

"Ronnie?"

Veronica looked up to see Luke standing in front of her, as physically appealing as ever, while she was doing a great impersonation of a homeless person.

She knew she looked like a deer in headlights. There was no other way to look. This wasn't a public place. Technically it was, but the public was out doing other things. She and the cowboy were alone.

He sighed. "It's only been a few days. What could have gone this far south in that period of time? Surely you have savings, friends, family . . . ?"

She didn't want to give him any information but she was sure the expression on her face answered all of his questions. He sat beside her on the bench, and she inched away, trying not to be obvious about it.

"Has somebody hurt you? Is that why you're scared of me?"

"No. You're a stranger. And we're alone. Isn't that enough?" She left off the part about him watching her, and probably following her, and all the creepy pieces that added up to freaking her out. It was more than a little weird that he was pursuing her like this, offering her a job when she had zero experience of anything that wasn't in a city.

"Maybe," he said, unconvinced. "Anyway, I want to show you something."

She jumped again when he reached in his pocket, but all he came out with was a phone. "I want to show you the ranch. We just set up the website last week. Would you like to see it? Maybe you could help keep it updated."

Veronica nodded slowly, not liking the way she was being pulled into his trap one answer and small capitulation at a time. He pulled the site up and handed her the phone. The sun began to set, and she was uncomfortably aware of that fact. It would be dark soon. She needed to get away from him and back to her room and the small bit of safety life still afforded her.

She flipped through the pages of the site, getting hungrier with each page. They sold grass-fed beef, as well as milk, cheese, and butter. There were pictures of food that made her want to beg him to take her with him despite the danger he posed. She'd been rationing money for food, afraid for when it ran out. Wasn't staying in New York the tiger? What if both doors had tigers of different breeds— grisly death either way?

"There are lots of things you could do out there. We'd keep you busy and well fed."

"Why are you doing this? I was a jerk to you, and I have no ranch-related skills."

He looked away, but she'd seen his eyes before he'd managed it. He wanted her. She didn't know why, and she didn't really care. It was pure animal lust, and going with him meant one way or another she'd end up in his bed.

"I just want to help you."

She handed the phone back to him, a chill going down her spine as the sun sank beneath the trees. She felt torn. A part of her wanted to ask him to walk her back to her room, but she didn't feel safe with him, either: then he'd know where she slept at night.

"I'm sorry, I really can't. I'll be fine."

He sighed deeply and stood. "All right. You still have my card?"

Veronica nodded. She'd held that card in her hands, staring at it for days now, wanting it to be a real safety net but too afraid it was a trap. She'd never been the woman who trusted pretty strangers. Women around her would get drunk at bars and trustingly go home with strange men because they were attractive, and therefore somehow safe. Veronica had never looked at things that way. Strangers were strangers. Men you didn't know were men you couldn't trust. And what did she know about men you *could* trust? Nothing. For all she knew, such men were a fairy tale.

"If you change your mind, call me. I'll come get you."

He started to walk away, and for a hysterical moment she wanted to beg him to take her with him. Judging by the way her house of cards had fallen around her, it was fuck him for room and board or fuck strangers. Stripping would be an option right before it got that dire, but she wasn't sure she could stand on a stage and shed her clothing while men ogled her. It seemed almost as bad as sex with strangers for money.

He'd gotten several yards away when he cursed, turned around, and came right for her. There was purpose and determination on his face that froze her to the bench, immobilizing her even down to her vocal cords. By the time she worked up a scream, his hand was over her mouth.

"Sorry, Ronnie, you're coming with me."

Instinctively she bit his hand, and just as instinctively he smacked her, but he didn't look sorry. That scared her more than anything else. He hadn't hit her hard, and didn't look like he would do it again, but the look in his eyes—the look that dared her to challenge him right now—was enough.

"Fine. Scream. My truck's not far."

She kicked desperately out at him, but he swept an arm under her legs and scooped her up. Even with her wriggling and struggling, he made it back to the truck.

He'd left the doors unlocked, probably something he'd grown used to in Vermont. Unluckily for her, some thug hadn't stolen it. She screamed one last time before he shoved her into the passenger side. Moments later, rope from the trunk was being tied around her wrists and ankles. He pulled out a knife, and she shrank back.

"I'm cutting the rope, not you. Relax."

Relax!?

"Ask again why I'm afraid of you." She couldn't stop the tears streaming down her cheeks.

"This is just so you don't hurt me or wreck us. That's it. Judging from the state you were in just a week after you were fired, if I left you, you'd die in a ditch or be raped in an alley."

"How do I know that fate doesn't await me with you?"

"Guess you'll have to start being nicer to me."

He took the second length of rope and pulled her wrists down and tied them to her ankles. The rope was long enough that she could sit up properly in the car, but not long enough for her to hold her arms up to get the attention of other motorists.

Five minutes later he started the engine. It was fully dark now.

"Just let me go." She tried her best to stay calm, but the act was failing miserably.

"No."

"Are you going to kill me?"

"Don't be silly. Why would I kill you?"

She snorted. "Why would you *kidnap* me?"

"Because you clearly can't take care of yourself. Now I've got a place for you where you'll be fed and safe instead of out on the streets like a crack addict."

"Are you going to keep me tied up?"

"No. I told you, I have work for you. You'll be doing work."

"Like hell, you cretin. I'm not your slave."

He glanced in the rear view and pulled onto the interstate. "Let me ask you something. Do you have any friends you can stay with?" He had to know the answer to that, given how he'd found her—assuming he hadn't followed her the whole week. He was just tormenting her.

"No. I have, or *had*, coworkers."

"Why don't you have friends? Could it be your charming personality?"

Veronica stared out the window into the night as it blurred by. So much for her lady or the tiger choice. She tried not to cry when she answered. "I worked long hours, so I didn't have time for much of a social life. What time I did have was spent with coworkers, and I never let them get too close."

"Why not?"

"I got into financial trouble and lost my penthouse. Status is a big deal in my circle. I couldn't let them know I was living in such a bad apartment. They aren't the kind of friends that would let you crash at their place, anyway." The walls around her personal bubble had dissolved in light of being kidnapped. Now, talking—making him see her as human—felt like her only shot at survival. He hadn't taken her to help her. He'd taken her because he wanted her. He'd come in like some barbarian and scooped her up as if she were the spoils of war.

"Are you still living in the apartment?"

She shot him a look. "No, I've been abducted."

A small grin inched up his face. At least it didn't look like a serial killer grin. She hoped.

"You know what I mean."

"No, I was evicted about a month ago. The day I got fired I had three days left there."

"So where were you living when I saw you tonight?"

"A hotel. Not a really nice one, but not seedy enough that I felt unsafe sleeping."

"I see."

They were quiet for several miles. Veronica decided not to waste her energy fighting him right now. Taking her across state lines was bad, but he'd have to stop for gas or a bathroom break at some point. If she just waited, she'd have her opportunity, assuming she could move like this or find something to cut through the ropes.

"Do you have family?" he asked.

"No."

"Dead?"

"That's rude."

"I learned it from you."

She sighed. "My mom is overseas. I don't even have her phone number. My dad left."

"When?"

"A long time ago."

Veronica sat perfectly still, reviewing the past few minutes of conversation. In her attempt to seem human, she'd made it clear what easy prey she was. No family. No friends. No one to miss her. She'd just given him everything he needed. Now he could do whatever he wanted with her and no one would make a call. No one would file a missing person report. No one would be looking for her.

"You should have had savings," he said. "With what you were probably making, there's no excuse for—"

"Hey! I don't have to listen to this shit. You're breaking the law, and you're probably going to kill me, so on top of that I don't have to listen to your stupid bullshit. My business is my business. You got it?" The shot of bravery was stupid.

He pulled the car over on the shoulder, and leaned in so close that when he spoke, his warm breath feathered out against her face. "Princess, you have to listen to whatever I say you have to listen to. I took you because I wanted you. All right? Sheer want. I rode up and rescued your ass, and when I'm finished with you, you'll politely thank me for it."

Veronica reeled back like she'd been slapped again. "Fine. I fucking hate men. Sandy called it. You bully. You shove your weight around. I never feel safe anywhere I go alone because I might come across a man like you. And even if I'm not around a man like you, I have to worry that maybe that's what I've stumbled upon. I can never feel safe walking through a park at night, or on an elevator with a man alone, or in a parking garage . . . "

"Who hurt you?"

"Besides you?"

"Oh, I haven't hurt you, yet."

The *yet* hung on the air, the darkest threat of the night so far.

Tears slid down her cheeks.

"Answer my question."

"No one."

He eased back and she could finally breathe again, then he turned the key in the ignition and pulled back onto the road.

Veronica woke with a jolt when the car door slammed. The clock on the dashboard indicated it was close to midnight.

"You fell asleep, princess."

"Stop calling me that."

The gas station he'd stopped at was deserted, with only one flickering light over the gas pump. The night clerk looked like he'd done his fair share of felony, so no help there.

"Are you hungry?"

She'd been hungry since Luke had found her in the park hours ago. She watched him, afraid to look any weaker than she already looked.

"I got you chips and a drink. You'll eat better when we get home." He opened both the chips and soda and passed them to her.

"Could you untie me?"

"Not until we get home."

"I have to pee."

"Not here."

"I *really* have to go."

"Just eat your snack. I'll find a place."

She bent awkwardly forward to eat, her tied hands making it difficult. She wished she was lying about having to use the bathroom. If he stopped on the side of the road somewhere and watched her, she'd die from the humiliation.

"I hope you like BBQ," he said. "I didn't know what kind to get. You were asleep."

She *did* like BBQ, but if he was starting to feel guilty for the situation, she wasn't about to assuage his guilt with a show of gratitude. Somehow in her mind, everything that had happened was her fault. If she'd managed her money better, she wouldn't have been so stressed and lost her job. She would have been living in the penthouse still, and she would have made a nice breakfast in her big kitchen with the island oven before work that day. Her path and psycho-cowboy's path never would have crossed. He would have gone back to Vermont without her ever meeting him, and she'd have a raise, and the coveted corner office with the giant windows and spectacular view.

As they drove and she ate, her mind went down other weird paths to Sandy. She wondered how Sandy would have taken this situation if she'd been in Veronica's place. Sandy would have stupidly taken the job, eager for the cowboy to take her off to his cattle ranch and *ride* her. Veronica shuddered.

"Are you cold? I can turn on some heat."

"No, I'm fine." Though she could admit in a sort of detached way that he was attractive, it was hard to see him that way when he'd taken her like he had. All she wanted was to escape and then punish him for demeaning her like this. Tying her up, treating her like part of his herd of cattle. It made her seethe with rage.

To her surprise, fifteen minutes later he pulled into a rest stop—not the side of the road. She was almost willing to be more agreeable given that he wasn't going to make her squat in a ditch to pee while he watched.

"This stretch of road is usually pretty dead this time of night. We are going in, and you will not waste time. As you've mentioned, I'm in the process of committing a felony. I have no illusions you'd protect me if someone stopped us. I'm taking a risk so you don't have to suffer. Remember that."

He untied her and rubbed the soreness out of her ankles and wrists. It felt like a prelude to how he planned to touch her later. He helped her out of the truck and followed her into the restroom, then leaned against the wall outside one of the stalls.

"Don't think about running. You have even less chance of surviving out here than you do in the city."

She wanted to kill him.

"Are you just going to stand out here and . . . listen?"

"That's the plan. Hop to it, princess."

"Just go ahead and kill me here. It'll save us both time and embarrassment."

"Did you just make a joke?" he asked.

"Maybe."

"So you trust I'm not going to hurt you?"

"What? No, I don't trust that. Do you think I'm that stupid?" She shut herself into one of the stalls and locked the door, hoping he wouldn't crawl under after her.

"I thought you were stupid for isolating yourself, not asking for help, and refusing help that was offered."

Veronica tried to relax, not believing she was in this situation to begin with. The fear had taken a brief backseat to the embarrassment.

When she stepped out of the stall, he said "That was all? Squirt squirt? And you're done?"

"I have a tiny bladder."

She looked at him in the mirror behind her while she washed her hands. He seemed momentarily distracted so she broke off in a run, glad she'd worn tennis shoes and jeans so she could move. Her heart beat erratically as she ran over a couple of hills and into the woods, more scared of the man at her back than the uncertain forest in front of her.

He yelled behind her, but she kept running. Trees came to life, their snarled branches grabbing at her, scratching at her arms, pulling at her shirt in an attempt to rip it. The trees might assault her before Luke ever got the chance. After a minute or so, the patch of trees thinned into a meadow littered with wildflowers—an unexpectedly beautiful sight in the middle of so much ugliness. She couldn't help looking up for just a moment. The sky opened out before her, vast and fathomless. The night was cold and clear, and the stars and full moon illuminated everything. For a surreal split second she felt more free than she'd ever felt.

Then she was on the ground, and he was on top of her, and she came back to herself.

"Get off me!" She struggled and wedged her knee between his legs, driving hard into his groin.

He cursed and eased off her for a second. It was enough for her to roll onto her stomach and scramble out from under him. Her hands dug into the grass for purchase as she crawled from between his legs. But she wasn't fast enough.

She let out a shriek when he pulled her hair and threw her back down to the ground, this time straddling her hard enough that she couldn't get away.

Her shoulder felt bruised from where she'd hit the ground, and his knees dug hard into her hips, pinning her with little effort.

"Please . . . " The word came out of her in a broken sob. It was the first time she'd begged him, and she hated herself for thinking it might not be the last. "Don't hurt me." The words were so soft she wasn't sure if he'd heard her.

He breathed hard. "Why did you stop running?"

She hadn't expected that question. At least he understood that she had to attempt escape.

"The sky."

He looked up, and if he hadn't had her arms held down, she might have tried to punch him, but the odds weren't in her favor this time. *Don't escalate the situation anymore. Get away if you can, but don't escalate. Wait for the next opportunity.*

But she feared she'd only get the one opportunity. And now it was gone, lost because she couldn't help being swept away by the awe-inspiring beauty of nature. No city lights. No city noise. No dark buildings threatening to crush her. Just the sky and the stars and a million brilliant tiny white flowers glowing in the moonlight.

"You'll love the ranch. This is our sky."

She didn't say anything to that because anyone who would do something like this had to be so mad she couldn't trust anything he said. He helped her to her feet and led her back to the truck. She didn't try to pull away; his grip was far too tight for that.

"Am I in trouble?" She didn't know how else to phrase it —how else to ask him if there would be retaliation for running.

"It was my fault for being distracted. You were going to follow your nature. But you won't have another opportunity like that."

When he got her secured in the truck, he noticed the bloody trails down her arms.

"Trees got you pretty bad. I've got something for that." He rummaged through the truck bed and came back with a first aid kit. "Hold your arms out."

There was nothing left to do but try to appease him and pretend she'd learned her lesson. He took a small bottle of hydrogen peroxide from the case and poured it over the cuts.

"Ow."

"Some of these are a little deep. It only stings for a minute." Then he did the craziest thing. He leaned in and blew on her arms, like a mother trying to soothe the sting on a child's scraped knee—not that she'd ever had that kind of mother. But she'd seen them in commercials.

Only one of her arms was scraped badly enough to wrap in gauze, but she still felt like a mummy when he'd finished. Then he got back in the driver's side and started the truck up.

"We're two hours from the ranch," he said, as if putting a fine point on the fact that her last chance to escape had just slipped past.

In the thirty minutes they'd been at the rest stop, not one other vehicle had come by.

It was two o'clock in the morning when they reached the ranch. The white house stood two stories with a wrap-around porch on the bottom floor as well as on the top, creating an extended second-story balcony. There were two doors on the second floor that opened out onto the shared balcony.

"The room on your left is mine. You'll sleep in the other room," Luke said.

"I get my own room?" She wanted to smack herself for asking that question.

"I told you I'd take care of you." He hadn't actually said those words, but he seemed to feel the implication had been heavy. "You'll get to see more tomorrow in daylight. It's late. We usually go to bed a lot earlier than this."

He came over to her side and opened her door. Before he untied her, he took her shoes. "Wouldn't want you to run off now, would we?"

After he'd untied her, he turned his back and went up to the front porch. "Coming, princess?"

Veronica stepped gingerly out of the truck and slammed the door. It was hard to see in the dark, even as big as the sky and as bright as the moon. She stood in the dirt by the truck, looking off into the night, wondering how far she'd have to go to reach rescue. She took a few tentative steps toward the unknown blackness and stopped, afraid to go farther in bare feet.

"Better than an electric fence," he said, as if she were an unruly poodle.

She took a few more steps away from him. The fear of what she'd encounter, what might slither over her foot or bite her, or what broken glass or rusty nail she might step on, was enough that she wouldn't go far, but his words had made it impossible for her to stop yet. Was she really more afraid of walking on the ground without shoes than of this man? So far, yes. That answer might be different later when it was too late.

"What are you going back to?" he taunted. "A motel room until the money runs out? Then where? On the streets? In a ditch? Under a bridge? Giving blow jobs in back alleys to buy groceries?"

She turned back toward him but didn't move from her spot. "Will I be doing that here?"

Luke looked thoughtful. "I haven't decided what you'll do, but I can promise you'll love every second of it."

Something low in her stomach twinged against her will at that statement. She turned back toward the blackness and took another couple of steps.

"There's nothing for you out there. There *is* something here. If you give it some time, you'll see that."

Aside from the tying-her-up part, he wasn't acting like a crazed kidnapper. He wasn't roughing her up or pushing her around or yelling or cursing at her. He seemed content to wait for her to step into the house of her own accord, but she wasn't sure she could do that.

Tears started to stream down her cheeks. "Give it some time? Just accept this? I didn't come here freely. You could do anything with me, and I'm supposed to be happy about that?"

There had to be a phone in his house. And if there was a phone, there would have to be an unguarded moment where she could call the police. But he was right. What was she going home to? Were the police going to give her a nice roof over her head and food? They wouldn't give her anything. But Luke might kill her or rape her. But did she really think those things were unlikely back in the city with nowhere to go? What about when the money ran out?

"What about the guys who work for you?" she asked.

"What about them?"

"They'll tell someone."

He laughed. "No, princess, they won't. We speak the same language. They'll take my side. So save yourself the trouble of resurrecting any high school acting technique. It won't do any good."

It took another twenty minutes before she could make herself turn toward Luke and the house. He leaned against the post on the porch, his arms crossed over his chest as if he had all the time in the world. When she started moving toward him, he turned and headed inside.

He flipped on the lights as they went through the lower level of the house.

"What am I going to wear?"

"I've got some clothes upstairs that will probably fit you."

"Whose?"

He was silent for a few minutes as if he were fumbling for a way to tell her. "The last woman who lived here."

"Did you kill her?"

"No. Get off this killing kick. I'm not a killer."

"Are you a rapist?"

His eyes raked over her. "Probably by your definitions, but not by the definition of any woman who's ever been in my bed."

"What happened to her? Did you let her go?"

"I don't want to talk about Trish." His voice came out clipped, and she dropped the subject.

Luke stopped at a bathroom tucked at the back of the house. He pushed it open without turning the knob, and Veronica realized the latch didn't catch.

"This is the only bathroom with a tub." He sat on the edge of the claw-foot tub and fiddled with the knobs, holding his hand under to check the temperature. "Come here."

Veronica froze in the doorway. "Why?"

Hard eyes locked on hers. "Come. Here. Don't make me ask again."

She took a couple of tentative steps into the small room. When she was close enough, he grabbed her wrist and pulled her over to the tub. "Tell me if the temperature is okay. Too hot? Too cool?"

The toughness leeched out of her as the realization of how much danger she was in finally registered. "I-it's fine.

But, I-I can't take a bath here. The door doesn't latch, you could come in, and . . . "

He stood, towering over her. He must've been six feet five and solid muscle. "When you're finished, you'll put on the bathrobe hanging on the back of the door."

She looked down at the tile floor. "Please, I-I can't."

"Honey, we're in the middle of bumfuck in case you haven't noticed. I'm about ten times stronger than you. I could have you at any moment I chose, no matter what you started out wearing or what you were doing, so get in the goddamn tub. I know you're tired and exhausted and stressed, just soak for awhile, and I'll make us some food."

He mercifully left her then.

She sat on the toilet lid while the water ran, and finally shut it off when she couldn't stall any longer. She heard clanging about in the kitchen. She'd have to bathe eventually. If the door didn't latch, it didn't latch. Did she believe she was going to be able to go long here with all of her clothes on? She'd seen the way he'd looked at her in the diner that first day. He'd no doubt been planning to take her even then. Losing her job was just an excuse for him to take advantage of a bad situation.

Finally she pushed the door shut and peeled her clothes off. She took a washcloth from a basket on the floor and wet it to wash the dirt off her feet, then she sank into the hot water, careful to keep her wrapped arm out of the tub. Whatever plans he had for her, he hadn't lashed out in anger when she'd run. Even after she'd kneed him in the groin, he'd only subdued her struggling. He'd tended to her wounds. How bad could he be? And he wasn't repulsive, at least, which was much better than she would have gotten on the streets.

Something deep inside her rose up, growling over the fact that she'd rationalize and stop at anything short of killing him. He couldn't do this to her. Whatever century he was living in, she wasn't his chattel.

A soap dish with homemade peppermint soap had been attached to the edge of the tub. She lathered up and closed her eyes, breathing in the scent, trying to calm her heart rate and form a plan. She jumped when the door was pushed open and rushed to cover herself.

Luke stood in the doorway in jeans and bare feet, his cowboy hat, boots, and shirt long gone. "That's a syndet bar so you can use it for your hair, too. It's got goat's milk and coconut oil in it. It makes your hair soft."

If he'd been using the soap for that purpose himself, he was an excellent advertisement for it. She flushed and looked away. "Don't look at me."

"I'll see you soon enough."

The tears started again, but he ignored them.

"I'm making burgers, so be quick about it." He shut the door softly behind him.

Her legs shook as she stood and pulled the drain on the tub. Whatever he planned to do to her, she wished he'd just do it. The anticipation was scaring her more than whatever he intended. She dried off with a towel from the basket and then put the bathrobe on. She wanted to put her normal clothes back on, but she was afraid he'd stop being nice. His kindness might be a mask, but the longer he wore it, the longer she lived.

Except for tying her up in the truck, he hadn't been cruel to her. He'd let her use the bathroom, given her a snack, patched up her scratches . . .

She tied the belt as tightly as she could, even though she knew it wouldn't stop him. The old hardwood floors creaked as she made her way into the kitchen. It was a throwback to the past, with appliances that looked like they were from the fifties and a green-and-white tile floor. The walls were a bright, sunflower yellow, and there were green gingham curtains on the windows. It was what she imagined a farmhouse kitchen would look like.

"Sit."

He brought over the burgers and some chips and sodas.

"Eat."

"Stop barking orders at me."

He arched a brow. "I saved you from starving in a ditch, I'll bark all the orders I want. Now eat."

Veronica stared at the burger. Every tiny demand she gave into was one step closer to . . . something. She didn't know what, exactly, but it felt that each time she did what she was told, they moved further along some plan known only to Luke. A plan to rebuild her? To unmake her? Part of her thought he might not kill her. What would be the point? If he were a serial killer, wouldn't she already be locked in the basement?

"I'm losing patience, Veronica." His voice had dropped a register, and it was the first time he'd spoken her given first name.

"What if I say no?"

"Then I'll spank you." There was no hint of teasing or amusement in his voice. The statement had been matter-of-fact as if it were an obvious conclusion that any thinking person would reach. What did you do with a woman who didn't eat her burger on command? Of course you spanked her.

She gawked at him, her mouth dropped open. "Excuse me? You'll WHAT?" Like hell he was going to spank her. She'd fight him until he killed her.

"You heard me. Eat your burger. There's no need for things to be unpleasant."

"Let me just say, you're about the creepiest little fucker I've ever met."

"Big fucker," he said around a mouthful of burger.

"What?"

"I'm the creepiest *big* fucker you've ever met. I'm six and a half feet tall. No one uses the word *little* when describing me. Eat."

She sat for another minute trying to determine if he meant the threat. The look in his eyes said he did. Was refusing to eat when she was hungry really worth dying over? Veronica took a bite. It was the best burger she'd ever eaten, and not just because she'd been eating cheap food for a week and had only had chips and a coke for the last ten hours.

"Now, you will call me *Sir*."

"Excuse me?"

He sighed. "Ronnie, you're making me tired. I've had a long day. If you interrupt me every time I speak, we'll be up until the roosters start. And they'll be starting in about two hours."

"That's before dawn."

"Welcome to the ranch."

She went back to her burger, trying to ignore the company and the fact that the way he was treating her, though offensive, was having a fucked-up effect. She was sure if—no when—he hurt her, it would snap her back to reality, but for now, his low voice, good looks, and semi-bar-baric ways were sending her spiraling back into fantasy world.

"You'll have chores here. You'll also be cooking for me and the guys. You'll keep the house tidy, and you'll tend to the garden in the backyard. We don't sell the produce; it's just for us. We don't eat a lot from the grocery store, some snack foods here and there and soft drinks. Most of our meat, eggs, and dairy comes from here or our neighbors and our produce comes from the garden. The growing season is short so we also have a pretty big greenhouse. Any questions?"

"I'm not going to be your happy domestic slave. I don't live to serve men." In real life she had barely been able to stand Joe as her boss at the ad agency. And she'd never called Joe *sir*. Her first two years at the agency it had been a woman, but then she'd run off to Australia with her boyfriend. The fact that Veronica would be the only woman here, waiting on them all hand and foot, caused an indignant rebellion to rise up in her. She didn't know how long she could play nice with this psycho.

"All right, get in the truck. I'll take you back to the city and you can die in a ditch or turn to prostitution and drugs to dull the horror of it all."

Would he really take her back to the city? If he meant it, she wanted to take the offer and get away, but his forecast of prostitution and drugs felt too true and close to the mark to take the bait. It might not be any better out there.

"Don't *you* intend to use me like that?"

"When the time is right, and I feel you're ready to be a good slut, absolutely."

She cringed at the way he spoke to her, rough and calloused like his hands. "What you've done and what you obviously plan to do is wrong."

"It's wrong to feed you and give you shelter and productive work?"

"That's not what you're doing."

"Isn't it?" He took his plate to the sink. "See you in the morning, princess."

Veronica was left alone in the kitchen with only the grandfather clock in the other room for company. She couldn't believe he'd left her unattended. Of course she wasn't going to run away without her shoes, but there had to be shoes somewhere in this house. Or a phone.

She scanned the kitchen, but all she found was a place where a phone used to hang on the wall. Searching the lower level didn't produce a phone either. She winced every time she stepped on the wrong wooden board, causing a loud creak to sound throughout the house. Luke leaned over the upstairs railing.

"If you're looking for a phone, I only have a cell, and it's locked in my safe in the bedroom."

So much for that, but she still had the other plan. She'd have to wait until he fell asleep. Even as she thought it, the prospect of actually making it back to New York sounded awful. So far he hadn't harmed her. What would be her fate in the city with such limited resources? Though by this point she could stand the humiliation of going back to Joe and begging for her job back, if the job still existed. She could see a credit counselor and get her life back on track.

If the slow downward spiral from her penthouse to the apartment with the ugly brick view hadn't changed her thinking, the past week of genuine fear for her ability to survive much longer the way she was going had. Jimmy Choos, Manolo Blahniks, and all the other frivolity seemed like just that.

She turned the knob of the door for the bedroom he'd assigned her. She was still confused that he hadn't thrown her down and raped her.

A silver, antique full-length mirror stood in one corner of the room. The wallpaper was a light blue-and-white stripe. The furniture was painted white: a chest of drawers, a vanity, a night stand, and a full-sized bed. The carpet was light blue to match the wallpaper.

Veronica guessed there was hardwood underneath. For a crazy second she wondered if the carpet covered evidence of something gruesome. The closet, also white, was filled with sundresses for the summer, both long and short, as well as jeans and sweaters for the winter. But no shoes. Not a single pair of shoes was in the closet or under the bed. A chill went down her spine. If she'd had any doubts before, now she knew—Trish had been a prisoner as well.

Three

Veronica waited until she heard the even hum of breath from her captor's room that indicated he'd fallen into sleep. She prayed he was a deep sleeper. She was careful to stay close to the walls, so the hardwood wouldn't creak. But when she turned the knob and pushed it open, the door gave a loud groan. He turned in his sleep, his breathing pattern interrupted. She stayed frozen in place, barely breathing until his pattern resumed. Then she crept into the room. If there were no women's shoes, she wasn't picky. Luke wore shoes. She'd just take some of his.

The moonlight came into his windows and fell over his face. Damn him and that face. That face had already made her hesitate a few times because something inside her responded to him. His mere presence did everything to her that her every sexual fantasy had done, but she was smart enough to know that the men she invented in her mind didn't exist—couldn't exist. She'd wasted enough time figuring that out.

She hadn't been out with a man since college. The whole thing seemed pointless. Men slowed you down. They complained when your career was going better than theirs. They wanted you to pop out babies and make sacrifices for the kids because aren't women all supposed to be maternal? Even in New York, you didn't have to peel through too many layers in a man to find the caveman underneath. All the equality and supportiveness on the surface was window dressing.

After her second abortion, Veronica had found a doctor to tie her tubes. He'd been against it at first, but given his conservative leanings and her past history of killing the unborn, he'd decided it would be best if she didn't get pregnant again. Smart doctor. Following that episode, she'd switched to women doctors for everything. Fuck the patronizing bastards who would give a man a vasectomy at nineteen but felt a woman couldn't know her own mind until she'd already had children or turned thirty-five.

For a fleeting moment, Veronica wanted to go downstairs to the kitchen, take a knife, and lop off the dangerous part of Luke Granger. While he hadn't hurt her . . . *yet* . . . she'd seen the perverted wheels in his head turning, and he'd admitted as much. She wasn't going to think about the brief inappropriate wetness she'd felt between her legs as the word *slut* had tumbled out of his gorgeous mouth.

Perhaps worse than that, he'd decided she'd be free labor around the house. He didn't seem intent on paying her. And even if he would, he hadn't given her the choice to refuse the job.

His boots weren't on the floor, so she went to check the closet. Behind the dark wooden doors, were his clothes and a large safe, but no shoes. Could he have put his boots in the safe? He'd put his cell in there. To be that meticulous . . . How many times had he done this? No matter what he said,

Veronica didn't believe he hadn't killed Trish and whoever else had been before her. This behavior was too pathological.

Somehow on the trip, she'd convinced herself that he was attracted to her and wanted to help her, and maybe the way things were out on the ranch didn't translate to more enlightened relationships between men and women. Perhaps he thought he was helping her, but since she was too stubborn to accept help, he'd had to take drastic measures—like an intervention with a drug addict.

She slipped past his bed to go back to her room when his hand shot out and grabbed her, pulling her back onto the bed with him. Her bathrobe bunched up around her thighs as he flipped them so he loomed over her. His hand slid up her thigh and between her legs, his fingers teasing just over her clit for a moment. It was enough to confuse her—to make her unsure if she wanted him or not. Even if her body did, she didn't. She hated him. He was the embodiment of why she didn't trust men. Weren't they all savages under the civilized exterior? Wouldn't they all do whatever they could get away with and rationalize it?

Luke Granger had decided he could keep a slave on his ranch and save some money. And past experience without getting caught proved his point. He sat up then and put her over his knee. It happened so fast she couldn't find the words to protest before her robe was up around her waist and his hand was coming down hard across her bare bottom.

She squirmed and struggled against him, screaming at him to stop. Indignant. Pissed-off. Humiliated. Scared. The threat of him was a reality now. He grabbed her wrists in one hand, the non-spanking hand. She would have bitten him, no matter the cost, if she could have reached him.

"Let me go you fucking bastard. I hate you. You are a sick motherfucking psycho who should be locked up!"

He ignored her screaming and kept spanking her until she'd reached her pain threshold. Her cursing and yelling turned to begging.

"Luke, please. I'm sorry, please." She didn't know what she was apologizing for. She'd say anything to make him stop. It hurt too much for pride to get in the way. In her mind, she reasoned she could just let go of it for one second to make him stop this, then she could reclaim her identity in the light of day when the pain had faded.

"You don't come into my room unless I send for you. Do you understand?"

"Y-yes."

"Yes what?"

She recoiled and resumed struggling, not yet ready to give in to the next step in her degradation.

"My hand isn't even tired. I can keep going."

Just the threat was enough at this point. "Y-yes, sir." If he didn't kill her, she'd jump off the balcony. "This is why I hate men. No one hurt me. But any one of you could have done what you're doing now. Isn't that enough reason to hate and not trust? How do I know when a man looks at me like you did in the diner that he isn't planning to act on his fantasies? I don't. None of you can be trusted."

He'd gone to stroking over her skin where he'd struck her. She tried to pull away when his finger dipped between her legs.

"You're wet. Dripping." He practically growled when he said it.

"Stop it."

"No. Say 'Sir, please stop groping me,' and I'll think about it."

"Never."

Another sharp slap landed on her ass.

"Sir, please stop groping me," she whispered through her tears. She was glad they were in the dark, because her face must be the color of a maraschino cherry.

He gathered her in his arms and held her, stroking her hair . . . *comforting* her.

"Please just kill me if that's what you're going to do. Don't do this on top of it."

"Shhhhh. The first week or so will be the hardest, after that you'll be happy with me."

He was insane. Completely certifiable if he thought she could ever be happy *obeying* him, being demeaned and degraded by him, reduced to a *thing*—not even a real person anymore.

"Was Trish happy?" she asked, her tone accusatory, but the answer he gave wasn't defensive or the one she expected.

"Very."

"Were you?"

His voice changed. Veronica was surprised when it came out choked. "Yes. You look a lot like her."

And did both of them look like his mother? Because that was in the serial killer handbook. Mommy issues. But she was far too wise to say that thought out loud.

"Go back to bed now. I'll let you sleep in since we were out so late." He kissed the top of her head and she went back to her room, thankful at least that she had a room away from him. The memory of his lips pressed against her forehead seared into her brain, keeping her from sleep for a long time.

Sunlight came in through the windows and balcony door, but Veronica rolled onto her stomach, taking the pillow with her to cover her head and block out the light. She wasn't yet awake enough to remember where she was.

Luke smacked her across the ass, not hard, but still degrading. "Get up, and make breakfast."

She squeezed her eyes shut tighter, as if she'd woken into another dream layer and if she concentrated hard enough she'd wake back up in the crappy apartment she'd been evicted from, or better yet, her penthouse. Being so tired, it was still possible to imagine that everything from losing the penthouse, onward, had been nothing but an ugly nightmare. After all, there was sun shining in her room. That had to mean penthouse.

What was the more likely scenario? That a Big Deal ad executive had gotten into such bad credit card debt she'd become nearly homeless and had been kidnapped by a rancher, or that all of that was a nightmare that mixed in a few inappropriate sexual fantasies? When she took the pillow away from her face and opened her eyes, it would be her penthouse with the spectacular view of the park.

The pillow was ripped away. She heard it hit the carpeted floor.

"Now, Veronica. It's nine a.m. That's practically sunset around here."

Oh God. She hoped he was kidding. The sound of his voice made her think that was unlikely.

She rolled back over and pulled the covers over her head. A second later, he'd ripped the blankets off her. Then she heard the unmistakable sound of a belt zipping through belt loops. Before she could react, he slammed the strip of leather against the mattress, so close to her leg she felt the air whoosh. She scrambled out of the bed, still wearing the bath robe from the previous night and crouched next to the night stand.

"I-I'm not making you and your sweaty pigs breakfast."

Somehow the sound of boots on carpet was as intimidating as they would have been on hardwood. He snapped the belt. "Oh really? I *will* use this on you. I'll strap those legs and then make you wear a short dress so the guys can see you've been a bad girl."

She held her hands over her head in a defensive gesture. "Okay, okay!"

Luke went to the closet and pulled out a short sun dress. "It only gets chilly at night right now, so you'll wear this today."

She balked at being told what to wear, but with the belt still in his hand, it was a battle she was willing to let go. He sat in the rocking chair in the corner of the room.

"Get dressed."

"Leave."

He snapped the belt again, and she struggled with the knot on the robe.

"There are underthings in the drawers. I prefer no panties, but I'll let you make that call today."

"Please don't do this."

He rolled his eyes. "Princess, you're in my castle now. You'll do what I say when I say. Pleading and begging isn't going to save you. All I want to do is look at you. Is that so bad?"

Veronica opened the drawers to find bras and panties. The panties were her size, but the bra was a size too small. She didn't want to think about the fact that she was wearing some dead woman's underthings and that most likely another unfortunate woman would wear these after her.

She slipped the panties on underneath the robe and heard Luke's *tsk tsk* behind her.

"I take it back. It'll be two rough weeks for you. It was optimistic to say one."

She shot him a dirty look, and kept her back to him when she slipped the robe off her shoulders and squeezed her breasts into the bra.

"Come here."

She paused, considering her options. She could say no or stay where she was and get hit with the belt, or she could walk over there to him. Either way he'd get what he wanted. She gritted her teeth and walked over to where he sat smugly in the rocking chair, his legs spread as wide as possible in such a chair.

He pulled her close so that she was standing between them, then he ran his hands over her, over the lines of the panties and over and around the bra, cupping each breast. She looked away as his rough fingers slipped under the lace.

"It's a little snug. What size are you?"

"36C."

She shuddered against him as he leaned in and trailed his tongue over the tops of her breasts. He pulled the cups of the bra back and rubbed the newly exposed flesh.

"You've got lovely nipples."

"Can I get dressed now? Please?" she said, trying to block out the feelings of arousal.

"Please *sir* can I get dressed now," he corrected.

She parroted back the phrase he wanted to hear only because it was the quickest route to getting clothes on. She wouldn't let him control her body like this.

He took his hands off her and nodded, and she scurried back to the bed and slipped the dress over her head. It was a better fit. She took a step back as he stood and moved toward her. He pointed at the door.

"Now go. Make breakfast. We're starving."

She turned toward the door and jumped when he landed a playful swat against her bottom.

The kitchen's long counter was lined with brown eggs that weren't quite the pristine quality of the grocery store and sliced bacon that stayed cold in a bowl of ice.

"There's biscuit dough in the fridge. I'll teach you how to make it, but what's chilling right now is ready to go. Just roll it into balls and put it on baking sheets," Luke said as he came up behind her. "Come." He took her hand and led her to the back patio, which was covered with trellis work and grapes. On the patio was a long wooden table with six chairs. "Right before the eggs are done, you can ring this bell for us. We like them scrambled." He pointed to indicate a sturdy wooden beam in the ground with a large bell with a rope attached.

"And if I refuse to be your house slave?"

"I'll whip you with the belt until you're more agreeable. And I'll do it in front of the ranch hands. You want to test me on that? I can ring the bell and bring them all in for a show. They'd be eager to watch that pert little ass get whipped."

Veronica shook her head quickly, knowing he'd do it. If he'd gotten away with doing this once before, she didn't want to think about the kind of men he employed, or how they might get off on her pain and humiliation. It was easier to just make breakfast.

"That's what I thought. You'll be making two meals a day for all of us, but the evening meal will just be the two of us. I'll show you the garden after breakfast."

Oh yes, the garden. She'd forgotten about her gardening duty. The joke was on him. She couldn't even keep a potted fern alive.

Standing on the back patio barefoot in a sundress, getting ready to make them all breakfast was the old-fashioned stereotype, minus one element. "I hope you don't plan on getting me pregnant."

"Don't be silly. You'd be next to useless to me pregnant."

A horrifying thought hit her and she couldn't stop the question from flying out of her mouth. "Did Trish get pregnant?"

"Yes."

Before she could ask anything else, he'd turned and headed out toward the cows, that ominous *yes* hanging in the air. What did that mean? She'd gotten pregnant, and he'd killed her? Veronica took a couple of tentative steps into the backyard trying to get her breath to come normally. She couldn't get pregnant; that risk was gone. But that wasn't the problem; it was the idea he'd kill a woman over something like that.

The grass was soft and well-manicured. She jumped at a low whistle, and turned to see a man that looked maybe fifty, a touch of gray starting at his temples. He was good-looking, but nothing like Luke. She mentally berated herself for that thought. For either of those thoughts.

"Well, ain't you a pretty thing? I coulda swore you was Trish for a minute. You like that grass? It's sod. We put it in for her. She was the damnedest woman. Couldn't get her to wear shoes for nothin' hardly." So Luke *hadn't* stolen her shoes? Or was that just the story he'd sold the ranch hands when he'd broken her down too far to protest the lie?

Veronica took a step back when the guy walked toward her, his hand outstretched.

"I'm Will. I won't bite ya, honey. Luke would have my ass. I'm in charge of the dairy side of the operation. We don't have as many cows for that, but Luke likes fresh dairy. We sell the extra. I'm also in charge of mowin'."

She tentatively shook his hand. "I'm Ronnie."

"Ronnie?"

"Short for Veronica."

He nodded. "Now that I'll believe."

She jumped again when she heard a squawk. She barely moved out of the way in time before a chicken could peck at her feet.

"Betsy's hungry. You'll be in charge of that. I'll show ya where the feed is."

"I-I thought it was just a cattle ranch."

"These are Luke's personal hens. Just enough for eggs for all of us, sometimes some meat, but usually we trade for that." Several other chickens made their way out of what looked like a little red house nearby. They weren't as brave and curious as Betsy. Will kept talking. "Hens are also good for the garden. We're all natural and organic out here. It's better for the soil, better for the animals, better for us."

She wondered if he was also in charge of marketing.

He hefted the bag of feed out of a nearby shed. "They're free range so they'll eat bugs and grubs. This is just some extra we give 'em, so not too much. Ya hear?"

Sensing Will wasn't about to touch Luke's *property* made her a little more comfortable around the other man. "What did he tell you about me?"

"The boss? He said you was homeless and needed a place to stay and some work. And we needed some help for around the house. Luke had a housekeeper come in for awhile, but it was still tough."

"Did he tell you he took me against my will? That he kidnapped me to bring me here and treat me like a slave, and god only knows what else he has planned?"

A dark smile lit Will's face. "Oh, he said you was given to melodrama."

"I'm serious. He tied me up and brought me here in his pickup truck. Against. My. Will."

"So you wasn't homeless?"

"Well, I . . . kind of . . . It's not like I was living under a bridge with some vagrants."

"But you woulda been if Luke hadn't brought you here . . . "

"Are you not listening to me? He'll *hurt* me."

"Nah he won't." Will took some of the feed and put it in Veronica's hand. "Just scatter that out, and they'll come runnin'."

She scattered the feed and the chickens raced over on their skinny legs, clucking and pecking at the feed around her. She would have been amused, if not for the conversation she was in. She had to get through to this Will guy and get help.

"He *hit* me last night."

Will broke out into a full-bodied laugh. "Honey, spankin' ain't the same as hittin'. You don't got a mark on ya."

Veronica's mouth dropped open. "Yes it is. You can't just run around hitting a woman like that." *Unless it's consensual*, the dirtier part of her brain supplied.

"Whatever you say dumplin'. I need to get back to work, and you need to get your cute little ass back in the kitchen and make us some breakfast. We're about to pass out from the hunger." He pulled a sad face.

He was already out of shouting distance by the time she could come up with a retort. They really were going to just treat her like one of the animals.

On her way back to the kitchen, she passed the garden, and a small man-made pond with a family of frogs around it. She shrieked when one of them hopped over her foot. If Luke wasn't going to provide her with shoes, the least he could do was not have chickens and frogs running amuck. In the city, not once had she been forced to encounter an amphibian or farm animal.

Veronica sighed when she reached the kitchen. She was getting pretty hungry, herself. And it was practically brunch by now. She almost felt sorry for the guys out there working on an empty stomach. Almost.

She rummaged through the cabinets and drawers for the things she needed and put some bacon in a pan and put the biscuits in the oven. While that was going, she set the table. There were six chairs, so she set six places, unsure if they would all be used. Then she put out some jam, butter, juice, and that milk would have to be last. It was in a large, clear, glass jar and had probably come straight out of a cow. It wasn't white like the milk she was used to, but had a yellow-ish tinge and a line of something thick at the top that looked like cream. She wasn't entirely sure it was good. She took a whiff. It didn't smell off, but what did she know? Her milk came from a sealed plastic jug in the refrigerated section of the grocery store.

In the city she'd gone out a lot, and eaten frozen dinners even more, but at least she could make a basic breakfast. That simple skill might keep her out of trouble for awhile.

Fifteen minutes later, she gritted her teeth and rang the bell, then she finished up the eggs and brought the food out to the table. The eggs had been a little strange—red spots in them. Was that normal? She was afraid she'd look foolish for asking so she'd just cooked them up.

If she hadn't been so hungry herself, she didn't think she'd have the will to demean herself in this way.

She'd already fixed her plate with a biscuit and straw-berry jam, some eggs, bacon, and orange juice. She wasn't about to touch that milk. It probably wasn't even pasteur-ized. She was already eating when the men arrived. If she was going to slave and cook for them, she'd fucking eat whenever she damn well felt like it. Unless Luke gave her that scary look again and ordered her not to.

"Will tells me you've met him," Luke said as the guys came up. "These other two are Jake and Robert." He didn't seem put off by her eating. If anything, he seemed impressed by her healthy appetite.

"Ma'am," they said with a nod, tipping their hats. Robert was about Luke's age and tall with a deep tan and sun-streaked blond hair. Jake had dark hair like Luke's, but blue eyes, in place of Luke's inscrutable dark brown.

This was surreal.

"Is this everybody? I set six places. There were six chairs."

"Trish always thought the table looked uneven with five chairs," Robert said.

Luke's face darkened.

"Uh, sorry, let's eat."

"Where's the maple syrup?" one of the guys asked.

Veronica looked up. "I-I didn't know. There aren't any pancakes or waffles."

"Ya made biscuits," Will said. "This is Vermont. Maple syrup with breakfast may as well be a state law."

"I'll get it," Luke said, scooting his chair back. "Finish your breakfast, Ronnie."

The men mostly ignored her during breakfast, instead talking about things she couldn't begin to fathom, speaking about machinery and tools she'd never heard of and what needed to be done before dark. She quietly observed them to see who might prove to be an ally. Who could get her off Hell Ranch?

Even as she thought it, she wasn't believing it. Despite the Neanderthal treatment, this place wasn't hell—at least not yet. The sun was shining and a breeze was blowing. When she finished eating, while the guys were talking, she watched the clouds as they lazily rolled by in the enormous sky. Part of her wanted to lay in the grass under it, but it probably wasn't on Luke's list of things for her to do today.

"Ronnie, we'll have lunch about three thirty. Just soup and sandwiches is fine. It doesn't have to be anything big since we're eating breakfast so late," Luke said. There was no condemnation there, just a statement.

"Sure, *dear*," she said, sarcastically. He was, after all, speaking to her as if she were his little farm wife who lived to do her part with the laundry and the baking.

Everyone dropped their forks.

"Sir," Luke said.

"Nobody else here calls you *sir*."

"That's because nobody else here is my piece of ass."

"I'm not your piece of anything." She turned to the others. "He has me here against his will. You're all accessories to kidnapping. Kidnapping is a felony. You're all going to prison when you get caught." She spoke slowly, careful to enunciate for the lower IQs in the audience.

"She's feisty. Good job," Jake said.

They all went back to eating and Luke raised an eyebrow at her. "Sure, *sir*," he said, not about to let it go.

"I'm not saying that."

"Who wants to see Ronnie get her ass blistered?"

The guys looked up, lecherous expressions on their faces.

"Sure, *sir*.".

Veronica got up from the table and retreated to the kitchen. She gripped the edge of the sink for support and let the tears fall. Luke was a fucking monster. There was no way she could live like this, and it was only going to get worse.

A few moments later, the kitchen door opened and banged shut. She didn't turn around, but she knew it was Luke. Somehow in the space of a day, she already knew the cadence of his steps.

"How can you treat me like this?"

He moved behind her, his hot breath on her ear. "How can you like it so much?"

"I don't like it. I hate it, and I hate you."

"Lies like that aren't very becoming on a lady." He slipped his hand under her skirt, pushing past her panties. She wriggled against him as his fingers pushed inside her, a gasp slipping past her lips. "You're wet. Let me tell you something about yourself, Veronica. You're in the girl's club I like to call 'methinks she doth protest too much'. Your indignant behavior over the slightest perceived gender inequality makes it almost certain that inequality is what you masturbate to at night."

He'd started pumping his fingers in and out of her. Against all reason and despite her fears about a grisly end, she moved with him.

"So this is all about my irritation over the stupid door at the diner?" she said.

"And you look like her."

Couldn't leave off that important point.

"If you were so into her, why did you kill her? Because she got pregnant, and you didn't want a baby?"

Luke moved his hands away and spun her around so hard she almost slipped. His eyes were angry when they met hers. "Okay, I'm done with that. Not that this is *any* of your business, but Trish died in childbirth. The baby was still-born. I lost them both in one night. I *loved* her. I didn't kidnap her, and I didn't kill her. If you think I'd kill somebody that looks like her, you're crazy. Bring her up again at your peril, princess. I'd love to spank that lovely ass again today."

"I'm sorry." Veronica looked away. She couldn't be sure if his story was true, but if it was, she felt like shit. Though, it still didn't excuse the way his mind had apparently snapped when he'd taken her. "Do the guys know you took me the way you did?"

"Yes. And not one of them will go against me."

"Are you sure about that?"

He nodded. "These men have been with me for the past ten years. They're my ranch family. They've got my back, and I've got theirs. If I robbed a bank, they'd help me hide the money. If I blew up a building, they'd deny it under torture. If I killed some people, they'd help me bury the bodies. So give up."

Will came in, then, with the juice and milk, followed by Robert with the butter and jam.

"Are we interruptin' somethin'?" Will asked. "We thought we better get this stuff back in the fridge."

"No, it's fine. I was just about to show Ronnie the garden."

Luke didn't ask for dinner until about seven o'clock that night, which he claimed was very late given how early they had to be up in the morning. Veronica didn't see the appeal in keeping this kind of schedule, or all the work involved. The late morning and afternoon had been spent cleaning, doing laundry and hanging it on the line, making lunch for the guys, and watering the garden, which thankfully was so late in the growing season that the plants were too hardy for her to kill if she followed Luke's maintenance schedule to the letter.

She'd picked several small tomatoes that had ripened on the vine for the sandwiches. After lunch she'd lain out in the grass, watching the clouds float above her, shifting into new patterns and shapes and merging together and splitting apart. Even when she'd been in the penthouse, the sky hadn't been like this. There had been too many buildings around.

Dinner was burgers again, more for expediency than anything else. Luke had showered while she'd cooked them on the grill out back with the last bit of light from the sky. When he came down again in just a pair of jeans, his dark brown hair still dripping water down his back, she tried not to stare. It was too wrong.

Twenty-four hours ago, she'd been tied up with ropes in the cab of his truck. There were still rope burns on her wrists, and a bandage on her arm from her escape attempt.

"What about the website?" She tried to sound casual about it. If she could get online, she could get out of here. Though even after such a short period of time, she felt less than excited about the plan. She didn't want to go back to the city, living in a motel she barely felt safe in until she ran out of money. She didn't want to go back to eating Ramen noodles and pork and beans. If he wasn't violent with her, would it be wrong to just stay?

"We'll work on it this weekend."

"Where's the computer?"

"Don't even think about it. It requires a network password, and I'm the only one who knows it."

"Did you go to college?" she asked. His manner of speech was relaxed, but still educated.

"I went to business school. I was going to open a tractor supply store a couple of cities over, but my old man got sick and asked me to take over here. I reasoned that it was a business, so I could still use the degree. And he wanted to keep it in the family."

Veronica picked over her burger, suddenly sullen. She shouldn't be making polite conversation with him and getting to know him like she'd been hooked up by an internet dating site. What had happened to her *women are people, too* philosophy? It seemed to have floated away with the clouds.

By dinner time, she'd worked up the nerve to hold a frog —out of curiosity more than anything—and had checked on the chickens in the hen house. It was hard to fight fresh air, a big sky, good, clean food, animals, and a cozy house. It was too contradictory to where her life had been just forty-eight hours ago when she hadn't known if she'd be eating in a month or where she'd sleep or if she'd be safe.

"Ronnie, in the end, everybody's a slave."

"Don't."

"I mean it. Do you really think anyone in this world is free? Everything is a hierarchy. Were you free when you worked for the ad agency?"

"Yes." But somewhere deep down she knew it was a lie, and that Luke was about to explain why.

He shook his head and took another bite of his burger. "You did good on the burgers. Eat yours before it gets cold."

"I'm going to get fat."

He laughed. "Not with all the work you'll be doing here."

She picked up the burger and took a small bite. He gave her a disappointed look, not impressed with the effort.

"You weren't free there," he said. "You had to work for money to pay your bills to live. Working wasn't an option you did just because you liked it. You were a wage slave. Just because it's packaged up like free will doesn't mean it's the recipe for happiness. What about your debt?"

"What about it?"

"How much do you owe?"

"Close to two hundred thousand," she mumbled.

He let out a low whistle. "Damn, woman. In some parts of the country, that's a house."

"I know."

"Well, you're free of that for now. I mean, I'm not about to call them up and say I have you."

Veronica looked up slowly from her plate as the realization that the crushing debt that had weighed on her couldn't be collected if they couldn't find her. Freedom. Or freedom after a fashion, yet somehow this seemed like a robbing-Peter-to-pay-Paul scenario.

"You don't have bills here. I'm not going to fire you. If you disobey me or I'm dissatisfied with your work, I'll just punish you, but you'll have a place to sleep and you won't ever go hungry."

She hated the nonchalant way he spoke of punishing her, the way he continually reiterated the dynamics and power structure of their relationship. But it wasn't enough for him to stop there.

"I rescued you. And very soon you're going to show me how grateful you are for it."

She crossed her legs, trying to push away the arousal his words created, spoken in that rumbling, gravelly tone. She'd meant to fight him more, but it had been so much easier to distract herself with the list of things he'd given her to do. But she'd pushed that out of her mind almost as soon as she'd seen it, as if she were forcing her brain to reboot. It was less scary to just cook the meals and do the laundry so when he came back to the house he didn't take his belt off.

That thinking made her sound like a battered wife, but so far he hadn't lashed out for no reason. Maybe he wasn't that crazy. She startled when his hand moved under her skirt, stroking her thigh. The words he'd spoken still hung in her mind. She'd wanted to be the girl who fought and clawed and screamed, the girl she'd thought she was that day in the diner when she'd acted as if he were some country bumpkin beneath her notice.

If things had been different, if she were still that Big Deal ad executive with a penthouse without a drop of debt, she would have fought harder, but he was right. There was nothing to fight to get back to. The only real fear was that he might kill her or harm her, but God help her, she believed his story about the previous woman. Veronica didn't even care that he'd taken her to fulfill the deluded fantasy of bringing the woman he'd loved back to life. All she cared about was that she didn't have creditors hounding her and the fear of homelessness hanging over her head.

She knew that one way or another, her body would be forfeit to someone, better Luke than random nasty men driving past *those* street corners.

"Okay. I'll do what you want."

He laughed. "That was never in question, princess. The only question was would it be the easy way or the hard way? I've broken horses. I have never ending patience with women."

After dinner, he took her into the living room. "Sit."

She picked a spot on the sofa and sat, unsure of what was coming next. She'd assumed they'd be going to bed soon. She wasn't sure if she'd be joining him or not. The idea tied her stomach in knots.

"I want to show you something." He pulled out a box with some old VHS tapes. Veronica hadn't seen anything but DVDs in years. It was an anachronism as if she'd fallen through a hole and had been transported back to the eighties.

From the couch, she could see that they had the labels on them that meant they weren't commercial videos bought from the store, but either things recorded off the TV or home movies. He thumbed through them and pulled one out and popped it into the VCR.

He went to sit on the stairs where he had a good view of Veronica, but none of the TV.

"Aren't you going to watch?" she asked, still not sure what she was about to see.

"No. I can't watch it. I need to watch you watching it."

He stood for a moment to flip the overhead lights on. Before, the room had been lit only by a dim floor lamp. He tossed her the remote.

"Push play and don't take your eyes from that screen, no matter what you see."

Okay, now he was starting to scare her. It hadn't occurred to her that giving in and saying she'd do what he wanted might speed up whatever his plan was. While he might not kill her, whatever he would do might have taken longer to work up to if she could have managed the will to fight him more, but a part of her had been afraid he'd get tired of her attitude and toss her out. It would be like biting the hand that was feeding her. The very idea that she didn't want her kidnapper to throw her out where she'd be subject to the whims of the elements was enough to make her stomach turn over.

She pressed the play button. There was a woman on the screen. She was naked, on her knees—a brunette like Veronica. Ivory skin like Veronica. When her face rose to the camera, Veronica could see the resemblance—it was eerie. Trish. There was someone else on the film. A man in black pants and riding boots. A riding crop dangled casually from his hand. Veronica couldn't see his face, but then he spoke.

"I want you to crawl for me," Luke said.

She began to crawl in slow, long circles across the floor, running the length of a large oriental rug, revealing a brand on her hip that looked like the image on Luke's business card. He followed, hitting her across the ass with the riding crop, leaving red welts as she continued to move across the floor. Finally, he stopped her.

"I want to look at what's mine. Show me."

The woman stopped crawling and sat back on her heels, her legs spread wide. There were a few tears sliding down her cheeks from the crop, but the look in her eyes when she looked up at him was pure adoration. She loved him.

"Show me, slut. Show the camera. I'm going to show this to the guys later. Would you like that?"

"Yes, Sir."

"Of course you would, you little whore. Now show me."

Her face went red as she spread her legs wider, parting the folds of her labia with her fingers.

Veronica looked away, too uncomfortable watching this with Luke watching her, wondering if he could tell how aroused she was becoming, wondering if it would seal her fate, terrified she'd end up branded like the woman on the screen.

"I said don't take your eyes off the screen," Luke said. It was the same tone he was using on the film.

She forced herself to look back at the video, afraid of what he might do if she defied him.

The Luke on the screen continued. "How badly do you want to finger yourself?"

A whimper.

"Beg me. You know how I like my sluts to beg."

"Please, Sir. I need to come."

"I know you do, sweetheart."

Another whimper. "Please . . . " Her finger edged closer to her clit and he smacked her hand hard with the crop, drawing a scream from her.

"Very naughty, dear. We don't touch ourselves without permission, do we?"

"N-no, Sir."

"Crawl to me, show me how sorry you are."

This must have been something they'd done in the past, because she seemed to know exactly what he wanted. She slunk over to him on her hands and knees like a beaten dog. Her tongue darted out to slowly lick the length of his boot.

"Good girl," he said when she'd finished ingratiating herself to him again. "You can touch yourself now, but if you don't come hard enough, there will be punishment."

"Turn off the video," the live, in-person Luke said from the shadows of the stairs.

Veronica pushed the button on the remote. She looked at the floor, scared of whatever was coming next, embarrassed he'd watched her watch him and her doppelganger engaged in something kinky. It was the kind of thing she'd suspected after he'd spanked her in his bedroom the previous night—and seeing the upstairs playroom while cleaning had sealed the truth. It was the kind of thing she would have fantasized—with him as the star—if she hadn't been so tired and scared.

The room was across the hall from the rooms she and Luke slept in. She'd discovered it while cleaning but had largely tried to block it out of her mind. It had a large black box on one end with a padlock on it, video equipment, a leather sofa, a pole that looked like a stripper pole, a few pieces of dungeon equipment, and of course the rug the girl had been crawling on.

A long silence stretched between them as Veronica waited, tense—she wasn't sure for what. An order? His hands on her? A question? Would he demand she tell him in minute detail how that video had made her feel? She didn't know if she could even put it into words for herself. If he *made* her do something like that, it would make the fantasies okay.

She'd fought against it, so strongly. What she'd seen happening on that screen—it would never happen that way for her. Of all the sex she'd had, it had never been pleasant, never like her fantasies. It hadn't even been good vanilla sex. It was just bad, start to finish, while she'd prayed it would end soon. She'd been dry, and it had hurt, but she'd kept going out with men, kept trying, like some nymphomaniac that pathologically had to fuck even though the act brought her no satisfaction. She couldn't stand to be disappointed again.

Had that been the start of her masochism? That tiny thread of pain that had accompanied her every sexual encounter? Without an orgasm, it had been the one thing she could count on. Comfort in the discomfort because of its familiarity.

"Go to bed, Veronica. I'll see you in the morning."

Her head jerked up, and she chanced a look into his eyes. What had he seen on her face that was making him send her away? Had he changed his mind about what he was going to do with her? She should be happy about that. And she was, but her face was flushed, and the space between her legs was throbbing so hard she wasn't sure she'd be able to walk straight. Crawling to her room sounded like a more feasible option, but she forced herself to stand.

"G-goodnight, Luke," she said. He hadn't moved from his spot on the stairs.

He held her gaze and shook his head in disapproval. "Goodnight, *Sir.*"

Something strange fluttered in her stomach at him still wanting the formal address. She didn't want to dissect it. "G-goodnight, Sir."

He simply nodded his approval.

As she walked past him, he slid a hand under her dress to feel the wetness sliding down her thighs, then he let her continue on her way. She wanted to melt into the floor. If he'd had any doubt of her reaction to his perverted home movie, it was gone now.

Four

The only light filtering into Veronica's room was from the full moon. She'd held her breath when she'd heard him come up the stairs, both afraid he'd come into her room and afraid he wouldn't. If he came inside, she was scared of what he'd do to her, or make her do. If he didn't come to her, was he rejecting her? Something in that scenario was more upsetting than it should have been.

His footsteps stopped just outside her room, and an eternity passed before she heard him change direction and go into his own room.

She let out a sigh of relief, but then unexpected tears slipped down her cheeks and onto her pillow. She was mortified. She tried to console herself with the fact that it wasn't her fault. He'd *made* her watch the video. But it didn't help. She still felt dirty. Once they'd crossed that threshold and he'd known without any doubt the things that made her hot, turning away from her was too humiliating. He'd somehow found her lacking.

The throbbing started between her legs again, and somehow the embarrassing thing she'd just experienced, mixed with the video into a new fantasy in her mind, with Luke's nasty voice in her ear whispering awful things while she rubbed her clit.

She jumped when a doorknob turned; her hand stilled under the covers. A shadow fell over her, and Luke entered the room through the balcony. She was afraid he'd notice if she jerked her hand away, so instead she pressed it flat against her mound, hoping the blankets would camouflage what she'd been doing.

He flipped on the light and stood over her. Before she could protest or find a way to covertly move her hand from between her legs, he ripped the blankets away to reveal her fingers underneath her panties and a nearly transparent T-shirt she'd found in the drawer. Her nipples must be erect and clearly visible through the shirt as worked up as she'd become.

"Did I give you permission to touch yourself?"

"N-no, Sir."

"Were you thinking about what you just saw down there?"

She hesitated and then slowly nodded.

"Speak," he said, as if he were training a small dog.

She wanted to argue and protest, to yell and curse at him. She wanted to throw a bedside lamp and watch as shards of glass cut the side of his face. Instead she said, "Yes, Sir." Her breath came out labored when she spoke.

She started to move her hand away.

Luke's eyes were hard. "No. Now that you've been caught, I want you to leave your fingers buried in your pussy. I want you to be very aware of what I caught you doing so you can't deny it later."

He retreated to the rocking chair in the far corner and sat, keeping his eyes on her. "Is this the first time you've had fantasies like this?"

"No, Sir."

"Take off your panties, spread your legs, and finish."

Veronica bolted off the bed and ran for the door. She turned the knob, but Luke's hand pushed the door closed, his weight pressed against her.

"You can't run from me, princess. Where would you go?"

"Please, I can't do this."

"Tell me why."

She choked the words out. "I can't give in. I don't want to be that girl."

"You *are* that girl. The only way you'll ever be satisfied is to embrace it."

"No."

"Yes." His hand stroked over her bottom, then before she could protest again, he slid her panties down. "I don't care if you're not Trish. You're close enough. You want the things she wanted. You're not going to run from me. You will do everything I ask of you. You will *be* her."

His words seemed to fall over her, hypnotizing her, taking her will.

"Do you understand?"

She wanted to scream *No!* She wanted to dig his eyes out of his head so he couldn't look at her the way he did, making dark things come alive inside her. She didn't want to be so twisted that she didn't care that he saw another woman when he looked at her, that some part of her wanted him to touch her anyway.

"Do you understand? You will *be* her."

"Y-yes, Sir."

He pressed her against the door with one hand while the other hand fumbled with his pants. For one terrifying moment she thought he was going to rape her, but then she heard the belt ripping through the loops. Suddenly that was more terrifying—especially in the frenzied state he was in.

"Please, I'm sorry."

"You're *sorry*," he mocked. "If you were sorry, you would have said, 'Please, I'm sorry, *Sir*'. I'm going to beat that fucking title into you."

"P-please, Sir, I'm sorry. I'm sorry, please don't hurt me." *He's fucking crazy.* "Why didn't you just leave me to die in a ditch?" She was sobbing so hard she wasn't sure if any of her words sounded like words any more. Out loud, they sounded like a string of hysterical shrieks.

She flinched when the belt hit the floor, buckle first. Luke scooped her up and carried her over to the bed, sitting against the headboard with her still wrapped in his arms. He held her cradled against him, his large, rough hand stroking through her hair.

"Shhhh, it's all right, Trish. It's okay, baby. I won't hurt you. Would never hurt you. I love you."

Veronica knew he wasn't playing a role. Something in her terror had penetrated the haze he'd been in. Now he seemed stuck in a flashback, convinced she was Trish. She couldn't stop crying, and he didn't stop reassuring her that everything was okay.

After a few minutes he slid out from under her, covered her with the blankets, and turned the light off. But he didn't leave. Instead, he moved back to the rocking chair.

"Go to sleep, Ronnie."

She wondered if he realized he'd called her Trish. The look in his eyes told her he knew exactly what he'd said. Though he may have had the best intentions with regards to her welfare, Veronica couldn't be sure he wouldn't kill her to exorcise the specter of the woman he'd lost.

The roosters jolted Veronica out of a dead sleep. Her eyes went straight for the rocking chair, half afraid she'd find Luke sitting there with a big knife and a crazy gleam in his eyes.

Against all odds, she'd fallen asleep before he'd left the room. She'd been afraid that if she closed her eyes, she'd never open them again. Even considering the kidnapping and everything that had led up to that moment, it was the most unhinged she'd seen him. Before he'd called her Trish —even while he was ranting that he wanted Veronica to *be* her—she'd been able to lie to herself. Rationalize.

There was a bathroom between their bedrooms with a toilet and a standing shower. She took a quick shower, thankful Luke had already gone out to work, and slipped some jeans and a T-shirt on.

When she got to the kitchen, there was a list of instructions for the day and a menu. Breakfast was going to be butterfly pork chops and homemade blueberry muffins. She hated pork, but the last thing she wanted to do was upset Luke further by debating the menu. With her luck, Trish had loved pork.

There was a knock on the kitchen door; it swung open before she could answer. It was Will.

He held up a thermos. "It's startin' to get a little chilly out in the mornin'. Luke said he made some coffee."

On the opposite counter, an industrial Bunn coffee-maker kept three fresh pots of coffee hot. He filled the thermos and started out the door.

"Will, wait."

He paused. "You need somethin'?"

"If I tell you something, will you swear not to repeat it to Luke?"

"Now, honey, I can't keep secrets from the boss. Luke is like a brother to me. How would it look if he couldn't trust me?"

"*Please*. He might hurt me if he knows I said something to you."

Will frowned. "I told ya he wouldn't . . . "

She decided to throw caution to the wind. The only way she'd get to tell Will was just to tell him and pray to God he saw the gravity of the situation and was smart enough to keep his mouth shut. "Last night Luke had some kind of meltdown. He thought I was Trish. I'm really scared of him. You have to help me."

Will avoided her eyes."He was real hurt about that. When she died, he almost lost the ranch. He wouldn't get outta bed. We had to pick up his slack and between that and feedin' ourselves, it was a rough few months. Did he hurt you?" Even as he said the words, Veronica knew he wouldn't believe it if she said that he had.

She wasn't sure how to answer. She didn't want Will privy to the thing that had almost happened between her and Luke. That was too private, and in many ways too humiliating. What had most scared her was when he'd taken off his belt and then called her Trish, proving he'd left mental health a long time ago.

"No, but he seems unstable. You didn't see him last night."

Will set his thermos down and went to the cabinet to get a coffee mug. He poured a cup and handed it to Veronica and led her to the kitchen table. "Sit and drink this. You need to calm down before you hyperventilate. I don't know what happened with you two, but Luke's not crazy. You can take my word on that. I've worked with him day in and day out for years and years. He had a rough patch after Trish died, but he's not crazy." The ranch hand seemed to be in denial about the situation, as if saying it enough times would make it true.

"Why won't you help me get out of here?"

"Just sit and talk to me for a minute." Will sat at the table and nodded to the chair opposite from him.

Veronica sank into it. "How long ago did she die?"

"A couple a years now. I never seen him so over the moon for a girl before. And when that baby was comin', I never seen him so happy. Usually he was all business about the ranch. Didn't have time to bother with no woman, even when we suggested he settle down to take a little of the load off us. You know what with the cookin' and basic homestead stuff. That's why I don't think he'll hurt you, no matter how he got you here. You remind him of her. He never coulda hurt her."

"And that could be a bad thing. What if he snaps and hurts me because he can't stand to look at me anymore? Sooner or later he'll realize that I'm not her. All I can be is a painful reminder."

"He knows you ain't her."

"Are you sure about that? Because last night, he didn't."

The ranch hand looked like he might waver, but then the kitchen door opened, and Luke walked in.

"Will, you taking a break?"

Will raised his thermos. "Just came for the coffee. It's too close to breakfast for a break."

"That's what I like to hear. Robert and Jake are bringing the new cattle in today. They got some good deals at the auction."

The ranch hand took one last uncertain look at Veronica and Luke, then he headed out the door back to his work.

When they were alone, Luke crossed his arms over his chest. "Why haven't you started breakfast?"

"I-I was about to."

He sighed and sat at the table across from her. "I'm sorry I scared you last night. I don't know what came over me."

"You thought I was her."

"I got lost inside my head for a minute. I know you're not her."

"But you wish I was."

"Do you want me to lie, Ronnie? I took you because you look like her. You know that. I'm sorry I lost control last night and that I scared you. I heard part of what you said to Will." He nodded over to the open window. "I was standing on the patio, and the voices carry out that window. I'm not crazy. I know who I am. I know who you are. And you and me aren't finished. It's going to happen, princess. I'll do damage control with Will. You make breakfast."

There went her only shot at help. Because if he talked to Will, he'd probably talk to Jake and Robert, too. By the end of the day, she'd look like the crazy one.

After lunch, when the garden had been checked on, the chickens had been fed, and most of the household chores were done, Veronica wandered to the end of the yard where the grass ended. From there, dirt stretched out with barns and pens until the ground turned to green again at the start of pasture.

She liked to think she would have protested more loudly about the work she wasn't being paid for in any other circumstance, but she'd seen off in the distance that the men worked harder than she did. Of course, they were being paid. Luke had made it clear he'd take care of all her needs. It grated that she didn't have her own money, but what was she going to do with it? Get into more debt? She wanted to believe she'd learned to be more responsible, but her recent cutbacks had been out of sheer survival necessity and the fear of going hungry.

And if she started spending money with her name attached to it, the creditors would line up at the door. She'd started to see herself as part slave, part fugitive, and the fugitive part made her wary about demanding her rights to a paycheck that debt collectors would just swoop in and take. Luke was right. Paid or unpaid, with so much debt, she was a slave, and there didn't seem to be an exit ramp in sight.

The work made the time go by faster, and it wasn't as if any of the men stood over her with a bull whip. Even if they'd wanted to, they didn't have time. Ranch life was hard. In the end, she had the easier end of things even without being a natural at gardening.Luke had given her a list of things to check for on the leaves.

Veronica was starting to suspect that people without green thumbs lacked knowledge, not magic. Gardening was something of a crapshoot and something of a science. The more you knew, the less gambling there was. But an outsider wouldn't know that. They'd put something in the ground, it would die, and they would assume they just didn't have the magic touch.

She stared at the sharp division between thick, green grass and dirt. She hadn't ventured this far before without shoes. Even the idea of walking in grass without shoes had seemed like a treacherous activity only a few days ago. Who knew what bacteria and parasites were in the ground? She took a few steps onto the warm dirt and then continued on, wondering if she was allowed out this far.

From a barn a few yards away, Veronica could hear a cow making a horrible, distressed sound.

"Hold him!" Luke shouted.

She raced to the barn door to see what was going on. A young steer was being held down while Robert clipped part of his coat away on his hip, then Luke raised a hot branding iron and seared its hide. Smoke and the smell of burnt flesh filled the air.

"No!" She couldn't help the protest. Luke pulled the branding iron away and gave her a look that made her fear she'd be next.

Veronica turned and ran back toward the house, trying to erase from her mind what she'd just seen. He'd taken that thing to Trish and marked her like common cattle. He'd never hurt her? The scarred flesh on Trish's hip from the brand he'd given her was proof to the contrary.

"Ronnie, stop!"

Luke's footsteps pounded behind her, but she kept running. Finally he overtook her, and she was in the grass, panting and struggling to get away from him. His gloved hands held her in place. "Stop it!" he shouted.

She was crying so hard it was difficult to form words. "People use ear tags now. You don't have to brand them. Do you know how cruel that is?"

He moved off her and let her sit up while he picked stray bits of grass out of her hair and off her dress. "You sound like one of those PETA people, or the lawmakers trying to phase out branding. That's their endgame, you know. I forget you're from the city and think food comes from the grocery store."

"It *should* be phased out. I'm not the one with the problem, here!" She couldn't stop seeing the calf struggling while Robert held him down and then the cry of pain when the hot iron hit its mark.

"It doesn't hurt them as much as you think. That cry is more from fear and shock than pain."

"How would you know? Are you a cow whisperer?"

"I've branded hundreds of cows. And I've branded a human. The danger comes in getting it too hot so it damages the tissues under the skin, or in not getting it hot enough to kill the nerve endings. Then it hurts for a long time. But like I said, I'm a pro at this. I've got a professional branding heater that regulates the temperature out there. I know what I'm doing. It doesn't hurt them. And it didn't hurt Trish."

Veronica thought she might be sick at the casual way he spoke of pressing a hot iron to the flesh of the woman he supposedly loved, to say nothing of all the poor cattle. If he'd loved Trish, and Veronica was a dim replacement, what hope of safety did she have with him?

"I don't brand them for the purpose of hurting them," he said. "It protects them from theft and getting lost. They wander a lot when they graze. Sometimes my cattle get mixed in with other people's cattle. They cost too much to lose like that. This is my livelihood, Ronnie. This ranch has been in my family for four generations. That's been our cattle brand for the same time period."

"Tags," Veronica said, still not willing to let it go.

"Tags come off. Sometimes the cows do it; sometimes hustlers do it. Brands are permanent."

At least in his own mind, he seemed to think his actions were justified, but the idea of him doing that to a human being when he had no practical rationalizations, made her feel like she was suffocating in a small cramped place, even though they were out under the open sky with plenty of air.

"What about Trish? There's no justification for making her . . . "

"She asked for the brand."

Veronica's eyes widened, not ready to believe him. What woman in her right mind would ask to be hurt and mutilated like that? Perhaps Trish had been as insane as Luke. Those two had been made for each other, cut out of the same cloth of crazy.

Luke pulled his gloves off and gripped her chin, forcing her eyes to his. "No, Ronnie. She *asked* for the brand. She knew what it meant, what it signified."

"That she was no better than cattle for you to use or slaughter at your whim?"

The slap across her cheek knocked the wind out of her.

"You're a monster," she said, holding a hand to the warm, red mark he'd no doubt just left on her. "I don't believe anything you have to say."

"You had that coming. I'm tired of the way you twist things."

Veronica scrambled back a few feet. He sat in silence for several minutes. Finally he looked over at her. The disgust in his eyes made her recoil worse than the slap had.

"That brand means something to me, to my family. Anything with that brand on it is mine until the day it dies. She wanted to be mine. I know the way you think. You have to understand that, no matter how much you deny it."

"I'll never be yours," she said, her voice laced with contempt.

"You *are* mine."

"No."

"We'll see." He stood and scooped her up, going back to the barn with her kicking and screaming in his arms. Her mind blanked, not allowing her to think about what his intentions surely were.

Two other cows were in a pen, waiting their turn. Robert stood in the middle of the barn. His eyes widened when Luke threw Veronica to the ground.

"I'm going to need you to hold her down."

She looked up at the other man, pleading in her eyes. Now he'd seen how crazy Luke was, somebody had to help her. "Please, don't let him do this," she whimpered.

"You appeal to me, not him, Princess. I'm the one who owns you. Do you see the big *G* on the branding iron?"

Robert raised one of the brands out of the heater, and she nearly went mad from panic seeing how bright red the iron was, then he laid it back down in the burner.

She turned to Luke from her sprawled position in the dirt. "P-please, Sir. You can't do this to me."

"Can't? Don't tell me what I *can't* do with my property. That won't play in your favor."

"I'm sorry." The tears streamed down her cheeks.

"Are you mine, Ronnie?"

"Y-yes, Sir," she said, hoping verbal surrender alone would end the frenzy that had started in him again. If he did this to her and she survived it, she'd show the mark to Will and make him feel guilty forever for walking away and leaving her alone with Luke in the kitchen. He could have taken her out of here. Between the mean streets of New York and this, she finally knew which fate was preferable: not this one. Luke was the door with the tiger behind it.

He grabbed the dress and ripped, pulling the fabric apart, leaving her in her underwear. She wasn't even wearing a bra—the ones in the drawer were so tight she'd finally given up on them. But she was too upset by what was about to happen to her to be concerned with the ranch hand seeing her half naked.

"NO! Please, please. You don't have to do this."

"I mark what's mine. Robert hold her."

The ranch hand studied her for a minute. "I'm not sure about this, boss."

Veronica made another attempt to plead her case. "You said Trish asked for the brand. Maybe that's true, but I'm *begging* you not to do this. Please, I won't defy you again. I belong to you, please. I'll never say I don't again." She was babbling, repeating herself, unable to stop the endless litany of pleading. Words that had seemed so hard to say a few days ago spilled from her mouth in a desperate bid for safety and protection.

"I also didn't kidnap her. Face it, sweetheart, there is a lot about our situation that is different."

"She's not Trish," Robert said.

"I know she's not Trish! Why does everyone keep saying that? But she may as well be."

Her face heated when he slid two fingers underneath her panties. "She's so wet right now. Do you want to check for yourself? She was born for this."

Veronica chanced a look back at Robert. The expression on his face had changed from pity and uncertainty to pure, animal lust. He was lost to her as an ally now. Apparently her body betraying her with arousal, no matter what *she* wanted, was enough to count as consent in his book.

"At the deepest core of her being, all she wants is to be owned and dominated. She wants to come, bucking like a wild horse. You didn't see her last night. She's not Trish, but she looks the same and she's wired the same. She should be marked the same. I need this."

Veronica changed tactics. "I'll never forgive you. I'll hate you if you do this."

"No. You won't. You'll feel like you belong to me, and it will be that much easier to surrender to the things I'll make you do."

She wished now that she'd masturbated for him the previous night like he'd asked. If she had, things might not have escalated to this point. All she'd had to do was obey—appease him a little. It didn't matter if it was right or wrong. The only thing that mattered was surviving his special kind of crazy until she could get away. A job at a strip joint was sounding better and better, but who would hire her with a cattle brand on her hip?

Robert sat in the dirt beside her and put her head on his lap. He trailed fingers through her hair in an attempt to comfort her while she cried. "Just try to be still. It'll be over in a few seconds."

How could he go along with this?

"Are you going to be still or are you going to try to fight, because I can't guarantee it won't hurt if you thrash around. And you'll mess up the design."

Inside, her heart was trying to escape its cage. He was really going to permanently mark her like one of his cows. She couldn't believe she was lying in her underwear in the dirt, being held by some ranch hand, waiting for a branding iron to strike her skin.

"Are you hearing me, Ronnie?"

"Y-yes, Sir." She turned to look at him again, the resignation starting to fall over her. "Do you promise I can handle it?" She wasn't sure it mattered what he said, but she was so terrified she'd take any comfort she could get.

"If your concern is pain, don't worry. Trust me for one minute. If you don't trust me not to harm you, trust that I've been doing this long enough to know how to do it. Remember what I said. Brands that hurt are either too cool or too hot. I know what the right temperature range is. Trust me."

How could she trust him? After everything he'd put her through already, extending an ounce of trust to this man was stupid, but what choice did she have?

A moment later, the hot iron struck her skin. She tensed, expecting horrible pain, but it was shockingly minimal. He held the iron to her skin for a few seconds then pulled it away. She turned to find a look of satisfaction in his eyes at having marked her.

Relief and endorphins flooded her as he picked her up and carried her back toward the house. Once they reached the grass, he laid her down and applied an ointment to the brand, then he covered her with her ripped dress.

"W-what are you doing?"

"I'm letting you ride out the endorphin rush out here. And I'm going back to work. Don't forget dinner by six thirty."

Veronica's head fell back on the grass as she looked up at the sky that went on forever. She felt like a cloud, detached from her body, floating up there in the big bright blue. Her breath came in and out in slow, measured sounds that lulled her like the hypnotic waves on the beach. Her college drug experimentation had been limited, but this was almost like being high. It was definitely an altered state. She couldn't remember ever being this relaxed before as the breeze brushed over her face. The leaves on a nearby apple tree became the most fascinating things she'd ever seen.

A small group of butterflies fluttered around in her line of sight, and she couldn't be sure if they were even real. When they fluttered off, she felt she'd become one with the tree, the grass she lay on, and the fluffy clouds. She felt open like the sky.

Five

When Veronica woke, it was to a burning sensation, but it wasn't the brand. It was the sun she'd fallen asleep in. She looked up to find herself lying in Luke's shadow.

"I didn't hear the dinner bell."

She scrambled to get up but felt dizzy from the heat. He caught her before she fell.

"I'm sorry, Sir. Don't be mad. I didn't mean to . . . " Why was she apologizing to him? Because she was scared. He'd literally scarred her for life while she'd begged him not to.

"It's all right. You've never had an endorphin rush like that before, have you?"

She shook her head.

"Then I shouldn't have left you alone."

She winced as he scooped her up and carried her back to the house. Her hip was sore from where the brand had struck her. "It hurts."

"It'll be sore for quite a while."

"You said it wouldn't hurt." She was thankful he'd covered her with her dress or a lot more of her would be sunburned.

"I meant it wouldn't hurt in the way you thought it would. You were expecting searing, agonizing pain, like a small surface burn only a lot worse, but brands don't work that way. It's not torture, even though it looks like it to outsiders. Not if you do it right."

When they reached the house, he sat her at the kitchen table and poured her a tall glass of water. "Drink. You're dehydrated."

She drank the water down while he inspected her. He pulled the dress she'd been clutching away to leave her in her panties, covered in dirt. Her arms, shoulders, and face had gotten burned in the sun. The rest had been protected by the dress.

"I'll be right back."

He hadn't yelled at her or done anything bad because she hadn't made dinner. He returned a few minutes later with a spritz bottle that looked like it had water in it.

"Close your eyes tight and lean your head back."

She was too drained to argue or ask questions, but she wasn't prepared when the strong scent of vinegar hit the air. He sprayed her face, arms, and shoulders until she felt like a salad. Then he patted her face with a paper towel to stop it from dripping.

"It'll help your sunburn," he said. "You can open your eyes now. Would you like to see your brand?" He said it conversationally as if she'd gone to a trendy body modification shop and selected the design herself. In reality, it was an ugly reminder that he could do whatever he wanted with her, and she didn't have the means to stop him.

She didn't know if she ever wanted to see it, but she said "Yes, Sir" to keep him happy.

Luke took her hand and led her upstairs. "I want you to take a cool shower and get cleaned up while I make us something to eat. It'll have to be grilled cheese and tomato soup tonight. What I had planned for you to make is too involved for this late."

"T-that's okay." She was just glad he wasn't punishing her for falling asleep in the backyard.

When they reached her bedroom, he stood her in front of the full-length mirror, turning her to the proper angle to see the brand. She thought she might pass out again when she saw it. It was dark red against her pale skin.

"It looks scary when it's new. When it heals it'll look something like what you saw on the video, okay? Just leave it alone." He brushed the hair out of her face with his fingers as if he were soothing her. She couldn't be sure if he saw Trish when he watched her reflection in the mirror.

Veronica looked again at the brand. If before she'd had even the smallest hope she'd ever be allowed to leave the ranch, that hope was gone, now. With an identifying mark like this, his crimes were painted across her skin, dark and angry—almost bragging: I did this. She stared at the G with the steer horns coming out of it that marked her as Luke's property.

She didn't know what to feel. She knew what she was supposed to feel: rage, violation. Instead she felt blank except for the throb between her legs. It started whenever he walked into a room now, whenever he came near her. Part of her would cringe away, tense, afraid he'd touch her, but another part needed him to. When she looked at Luke again, he was staring at his mark, an unapologetic smile curving his lips.

"This is wrong. I didn't ask for any of this. You do know the difference, right?"

"I saved you," he said simply, still convinced anything he did to her was okay because she was going to end up on the streets anyway. "Run along and get in the shower. I'll bring you something to wear."

She drifted to the upstairs bathroom in a fog. Maybe she was in shock. Or maybe it was the low-level constant buzz of arousal she'd felt from the moment she'd entered his presence—something she'd ignored as best she could until Luke had pointed it out so many times. Her face burned—more from embarrassment than the sunburn—over Luke so casually sliding his fingers inside her panties in full view of the ranch hand. She'd been too afraid at the time of what he was about to do to her, but now in the house, she didn't think she'd be able to look at the guy at breakfast tomorrow.

A few minutes later, Luke came in with a white cotton nightgownin his hand. The gown had thin straps and was a thin enough material thatit would leave little to the imagination.

Veronica tried to cover herself. He arched an eyebrow and put the gown down on the counter.

"How long are you going to be so shy around me?"

It seemed ludicrous with what was the equivalent of his family crest burned into her hip and all he'd seen of her already, but she couldn't help the natural inclination to protect her modesty.

She expected him to leave the clothes and go. Instead, he pulled her arms from her chest and ran his fingertips over her nipples and the full, roundness of her breasts, as if testing their weight. His hand roamed across her flat belly and to the mound between her legs. He stroked her already swollen clit, and she spread her legs as her hips arched up to meet him.

"The brand makes such a difference in you. You know you're not going anywhere, now. Better to just open to me.

Give in. We aren't in the city anymore. There's nothing you have to fight for, here. I'm going to be inside you tonight. So get used to that idea."

A tear slid down her cheek as he rubbed her harder. Despite everything, her orgasm was building. It was confusing and exposing. She never had orgasms *with* men. It had always been later, on her own. She'd faked more orgasms than she'd wanted to admit to. Even the ones who had tried to touch her in just the right way had left her cold.

But then, no one had touched her like Luke was touching her. He touched her like she'd been brought into the world solely for his use, like her entire existence was meant to please him. The proprietary way he stroked her was clearly the only way she could come.

Luke didn't ask *is this okay? Is this how you like it?* He touched her the way he liked it, and she was forced to run along behind him, panting and hungry for more.

He pulled his hand away from her.

"Please . . . "

"I need to make us some food. Take your shower, and put the nightgown on. No panties or I'll be very unhappy."

As soon as he'd pulled the door shut, her fingers slipped between her legs to finish. The door opened again, his gaze causing her to shrink back like a violet. "And no touching yourself. You only masturbate for an audience from now on." He stared her down until she took her fingers from her clit. Then he left her.

For an audience? Did he mean him or him and the guys? Robert hadn't seemed shocked when Luke had touched her in the barn, and he'd known about Trish's brand. The threat on screen about showing the video to the guys that had gotten the woman all hot and bothered hadn't just been dirty talk. No wonder no one wanted to help Veronica. They wanted a piece of the action.

When she got to the kitchen, Luke was sitting at the table, his legs sprawled out, looking relaxed and expectant. Behind him, the sandwiches sat on the counter wrapped in aluminum foil and paper towels to keep the heat in longer. The soup simmered on the back burner, bowls and spoons already on the counter. Iced tea was poured and on the table with a couple of lemon wedges from the lemon tree in the greenhouse.

There was a darkly erotic glint in Luke's eyes. "How hungry are you, princess? What are you willing to do to be allowed to eat?"

She didn't know if he'd really let her go to bed hungry if she didn't do whatever he wanted. She'd always had the suspicion his punishments would be more direct and terrifying.

Veronica looked at the floor tiles, unable to maintain eye contact for long.

"Answer me, princess."

"I-I'll do whatever you want."

"Come to me on your hands and knees."

There must have been resistance on her face because he said, "Don't think, just do it."

She crouched to the ground and crawled over to him. She was painfully aware of what had happened in the barn each time she moved, the ache radiating through her hip. Inexplicably, the reminder that she belonged to him made her hotter. Crazy or not, it was hard to be near him and be anything but aroused for long. He was too beautiful in that rugged way. She stopped when she was between his legs. He unzipped his pants and his cock sprang free. Her tongue darted out to lick her lips.

"How many men have you sucked?"

The question took her off guard. "I . . . um . . . " If she told him the truth, she'd sound like a virgin. None of the men she'd been with had inspired the activity. In her fantasies it had seemed hot and exciting—helpless in an erotic way. In reality it was too demeaning. She'd never been able to be the Cosmo girl who could successfully pretend she liked or wanted a cock in her mouth.

"How many?"

"I don't do that."

"Well, you seem excited enough about doing it now."

She blushed and was thankful he wouldn't be able to see it for her sunburn.

"How many men have you fucked?"

It had been awhile, but in college . . . She did the math in her head.

"And I want the real number. Not the number women give men to appear more virginal. I'll know if you're lying."

"Thirty-four."

He smirked and spread his legs a little farther. "I knew you were a slut. Well, don't just stare at it."

Veronica inched forward and ran her tongue over the shaft. His hand tangled in her hair and he pulled hard, jerking her face up.

"I know you can do better. Pretend it's the only thing you're getting for dinner. And no teeth."

She may not have ever sucked a cock, but she'd seen it done. It wasn't a great mystery—she'd just never felt compelled to pretend she liked it. But Luke didn't care if she liked it or not. He was going to get off in her mouth either way. That thought sent an electrical zap through her stomach as she took him into her mouth.

His hand moved to the back of her neck and he pulled her in closer, going deeper. When her gag reflex activated, she instinctively relaxed her throat to let more of him in.

"That's good, princess. Surprisingly good, actually."

When he came, he held her in place so she could do nothing but swallow the thick, hot liquid. Then the kitchen door opened. She jerked away, and some of his cum slid down her chin and neck.

"Stay down," he ordered as he zipped up, pointing at her as if she were a disobedient dog.

She kept her eyes on the floor, unable to look up at the person who'd come in.

"Sorry, I left my hat on the counter after lunch," Will said. Footsteps receded to the other end of the kitchen, paused a moment, then came to stop a few feet from her. Veronica could just see the tips of his boots.

"Luke told me he branded you, honey. I'm real sorry I missed that."

"Do you want to see it?" Luke asked.

Veronica looked up in time to see the hungry expression in the ranch hand's eyes. "You know I do. Don't tease me."

Luke nudged her with his knee. "Be a good girl and go show him. If thirty-four other men have already seen you naked, it shouldn't be a problem."

She wanted to melt through the floor.

Will let out a low whistle. "Filthy little thing."

"Yes," Luke said. "She's been holding out on us."

Veronica forced herself to walk the few paces to Will, unable to meet his eyes. She could feel her nipples pebbling against the material of the nightgown and knew without looking that his gaze must be drawn to them. When she reached him, she turned away and lifted the nightgown to show him the mark, aware he'd get a view of much more without panties.

"That looks real nice. It should heal up good. She's our good little cow." He stroked the back of her neck.

"*My* good little cow," Luke said. "You only touch her if I'm around."

Then Will's hands were on more private areas, cupping and stroking her bottom—as if that were an invitation. She looked over at Luke, but the heated look he gave her made her wither and wouldn't let her pull away from the groping hands. She felt Will's wedding ring slide against her flesh and wondered what his wife would think about this.

He moved his hands to her front and pulled her flush against him. His erection strained through his jeans, pressing between the cleft of her cheeks. "You feel that honey? That's how bad I want inside you. Maybe the boss'll let me one day soon."

He pressed a finger inside her, and she wondered how far Luke would let him take this. "Jesus, she's wet."

"Fantastic, isn't it?"

Veronica closed her eyes and imagined it was Luke's finger inside her, not bothering to think about why that was all wrong, too. She rocked against him, not resisting as he pushed deeper inside, exploring her body like it was his instead of Luke's.

"That's enough," Luke said when the ranch hand had taken her to the brink. "Her first orgasm at the ranch is coming from me."

"Well, hurry the hell up," Will said. "Now I'll have to fuck Frieda." He let go of her and the kitchen door banged shut on his way out.

Luke went to the stove to pour the soup and bring the sandwiches.

"Sit and eat your dinner."

After they'd eaten, Luke leaned back in his chair, his fingers laced behind his head, watching her. She felt like an experiment.

"Will really likes you," he commented. "So do the other two."

Veronica stared at her empty soup bowl, wishing there was still something in there to distract her. She tried to keep her voice steady when she spoke. "A-are you going to share me?"

"We'll see."

"Did you share Trish?" Every time she mentioned the other woman's name, she feared he'd have some kind of meltdown, but he remained stoic.

"Often. She got off on it. I think you'd get off on it, too."

She didn't reply. Anything she said would damn her in some way. The ranch hand had felt how wet she'd gotten. She'd been thinking about Luke at the time, but did that matter? Luke had been watching, which had only aroused her further. That assessing stare of his as he dispassionately observed another man running his hands all over her, knowing she'd submit to avoid his wrath. It had started that deep longing she'd begun to feel for him.

He'd been intent on building a new Trish since he'd seen Veronica in the diner, and she'd fallen right into it. The part of her that wanted to fight and hate him and everything else with a dick had been beaten down by the carnal part that wanted to surrender. In all her sexual encounters, no one else had made her want to surrender, or kneel, or beg. All Luke had had to do was take her shoes, put her in a dress, and shove her in the kitchen with a group of men to wait on. She didn't want to think about what that said about her.

Veronica looked up to find him still staring at her in that assessing way. She wished she could know what he was thinking, or how much of her own thoughts he'd guessed.

His chair scraped back against the linoleum. "Wash the dishes, then come to my room. I want you naked."

Her heart was in her throat as she watched him leave the room. She filled the sink with warm, sudsy water and tried to make washing the dishes take as long as possible. The feminist on her shoulder insisted she must be offended and feel violated even over the dishes, to say nothing of anything else that had transpired. She should make another escape attempt, even in the dark without shoes. All she had to do was make it to another person. The evidence that would lead them to her kidnapper was burned into her now.

Whoever might know and respect Luke Granger, his family, their ranch's history—there was no denying who that brand belonged to. On her other shoulder was her slut side, the part of her that had tried and tried to be satisfied, now faced with the embodiment of all her sexual fantasies, no matter how wrong. It was the wrongness that made her so wet and hot to begin with. If the things she'd thought about were tame and family friendly, they wouldn't make her come so hard.

Her hands felt around in the soapy water for the next dish, but they were all on the counter now, drying. She pulled the plug to drain the water and dried her hands.

"Veronica, sweetheart, do you believe it's wise to keep me waiting?"

She'd shed the gown in the hallway before coming in. Luke leaned against the headboard of his bed, a white sheet draped carelessly over his tanned, naked body.

"N-no, Sir." She'd give anything to get rid of that weak stutter he caused every time she got scared.

"The dishes took twenty minutes. With the little that was there to clean, it shouldn't have taken longer than ten."

He pulled the sheet away to reveal his belt—or one of them—lying across his stomach. His cock was hard and ready to go again. She wasn't sure if it was over the prospect of beating her or fucking her. "Go across the hall into the playroom and kneel in the middle of the rug. When I get in there, I want your forehead on the rug, and your arms stretched out in front of you, palms up." When she hesitated, he said, "Now."

She waited in that position in the other room for what felt like forever. Every time she heard floorboards creak outside the door, she tensed. But each time, nothing. Finally, when she thought she'd faint from the fear, the doorknob turned and he stepped into the room.

"That was twenty minutes, Ronnie. Do you see how much time that is?"

"Y-yes, Sir."

"I'm going to whip you with the belt for making me wait so long. I'll be lenient and only give you ten. Thank me for that kindness."

"P-please, I'm sorry, Sir." She cringed as he circled her, stopping behind her where she couldn't see him."

"Begging won't help you. Take your punishment and learn from it."

"You're a motherfucking psycho," she said.

He jerked her back by her hair. "What was that?"

"You heard me. You are a sick fuck and everybody here knows it. The only reason you feel normal is that the guys who work for you are sick fucks, too. Do you want to ask again who hurt me? You, them, every cretin in the universe who'd even have the fantasy, let alone act on it."

His eyes flashed. "Don't get high and mighty with me. You have the same needs I have. Don't act like mine are vile while yours are enlightened."

"Trish consented. You *took* me. I never said I wanted this with you."

"Your body said it."

"That doesn't count."

He flipped her onto her back, straddling her, inches from penetration, but instead, he pushed a finger inside her.

"So fucking wet. Tell me to stop, Ronnie."

She looked away, her hips bucking against his wriggling finger.

"Please . . . "

"Please what, princess? Please stop? Please keep going? Please treat me like the livestock I am?"

"Fuck you."

"Fuck you isn't stop. Fuck you sounds like an invitation to me." He'd found her g-spot. No matter how much she wanted to stop him, her body craved the way he rubbed that little place inside her. When she didn't protest, he withdrew his fingers. "Get back in the position I told you to be in."

She scrambled back onto her knees. "Would it have made a difference if I'd said stop?"

"Guess you'll never know. That brand on your hip is going to be sore for at least a month. It should be a good, constant reminder of who owns you. Stop and think about that little twinge of pain the next time you want to open your mouth and say something smart."

She shrieked when the first lash landed on her bottom, sending a lick of fire across her flesh, strangely more painful than the branding. She tensed before each blow, terrified he'd slip and hit the brand, but he didn't. He was silent as he meted out the punishment, the only sound in the room her sobs. By the time he'd finished with her, she only wished those nerve endings could die like the ones the brand had burned away, But then he rubbed over her welted bottom.

"Get up on your hands and knees," he snarled in her ear.

Veronica raised up on all fours and then he was inside her, pounding her so hard she couldn't catch her breath. She was convinced she couldn't come this way, but the orgasm nearly ripped her open from the inside, tearing a scream from her throat.

She crumpled to the floor, still shaking when he pulled out of her. Luke rolled onto his back and pulled her against him. He was quiet for a long time.

"Are you on birth control?"

Brilliant time to ask.

"My tubes are tied."

He sat up, startled. "Why?"

"Why not? I don't want babies."

"Good."

She knew he was thinking about Trish.

A few minutes later he got up and left the room. She waited, but when he didn't return she went to his room. When she opened the door, he stopped her.

"Sleep in your room. My room is for good sluts that know their place."

"You're really mean."

"Give me one week, Ronnie. One week without resistance, doing anything I ask without question or begging or name calling and yelling. One week without fighting me. You might be surprised by how kind I can be, but my favor must be earned."

Veronica didn't reply. She just stomped off to her room and slammed the door. Once in bed, she tossed and turned, Luke's *Give me one week, Ronnie*, bumping up against Joe's *Give me anything, Ronnie* from the day she'd lost her job.

Everything inside her rebelled at the thought of submitting completely to Luke. It would be admitting he'd broken her, or giving him permission to do horrible things to her just because it turned her body on. But what if? Hadn't he already shown her glimmers of kindness? Wouldn't it be better if she had more of that, instead of the belt and the brand?

Would he have branded her if she hadn't said what she'd said about Trish?

Six

Veronica woke with a pleasant soreness between her legs, and a less pleasant soreness on her hip. The previous day's emotional and physical roller coaster came crashing back to her like a bad hangover. The last words Luke spoke to her the night before still hung in the air.

She couldn't stop thinking *Please be kind to me. Please help me survive this.* Like a mantra over and over in her head, as if he could hear her if she thought it enough. As if he might care.

He couldn't let her go now, not with plausible deniability. She struggled to find a way to give in to him, to erase her mind and just be her body, which seemed to know instinctively how to please him and submit.

She thought back to the day before, lying in the grass after he'd branded her, the feeling of bliss like everything was right with the world. Everything and everyone was in its place. Everything was as it should be. Life was a rich, interwoven tapestry of which she and Luke were only tiny threads. Nothing was a big enough deal to fight over.

When you became everything and everything became you, what was there to dispute? Everything just was. She wanted to go back to that moment and live there.

As she showered and made breakfast, she tried to find that quiet space inside herself that didn't cling and claw and fight and scream, that just drifted and merged with the clouds. That just ate and breathed and slept and fucked and everything in between any of that was just noise.

At breakfast, she was still trying to find this place when Luke said her name.

"Ronnie, come here."

She looked up, the flood of fear she'd pushed away coming back in full force. It wasn't what he said. It was the way he said it. That voice. It was ruthless and unrelenting. Anything said with that voice would bring her the greatest pleasure, the greatest pain, or the greatest humiliation. Most likely all three. She wanted to run from that voice and never look back. The only problem was that while she was running, she was likely to circle back and run toward it again —his inexplicable pull on her was that strong.

She scooted her chair back and went to him. His hand, ran over her bottom through the sundress she'd put on.

"Are you wearing panties?"

The men stopped eating, forks clanging against plates as they fell. They looked at her, waiting. It didn't appear odd to them that the question was being asked. They just wanted to hear the answer.

"Yes, Sir," she said, finally killing the stutter. It could still come back. It was early yet.

"That disappoints me. Take them off."

What was the point? Nothing she did would ever be good enough. She'd never be Trish, even if she followed his orders to the letter every moment for the rest of her life.

Where had that come from? She pushed past the urge to fight him on the panty issue and turned to go inside.

"Take them off here."

If she begged him, he'd only humiliate her worse. He might punish her. *Just give in. Whatever he wants. Just do it.* He'd said the first week or so was the hardest. Had it been hard for Trish? Even if he hadn't taken her against her will? Was it something Veronica would have had to push through either way?

She wanted him. She wanted to live out every filthy fantasy she'd ever had with him, but she couldn't get past the fact that she hadn't come here freely. She almost had. In that park when she'd been so desperate for anything to make her life better and he'd given her one more chance to go with him, what if she'd just gone, with no ropes or terror?

What if she'd taken the work as just a matter of course? What if they'd agreed that room and board was sufficient pay for a few household chores and meal preparation? What if he'd seduced her and she'd fallen under his spell? Would it really be easier to go down the dark and gnarled path he was taking her down?

"Veronica . . . " His voice had taken on that edge again. It was the way he sounded only a few moments before consequences.

She balanced with one hand against the table and lifted the dress to reach the top of her panties and took them off without thinking it through. She was about to go back to sit down—a wildly optimistic choice—when his hand covered hers, stopping her.

A look passed between him and the guys, and as if they'd done this all before, they stacked the plates at the far end of the table, where the extra chair sat. Trish may have decided on six chairs to keep the table even, but each day, that last empty chair at the end of the table felt like the place for the ghost of his former lover.

Luke grabbed Veronica's wrist and pulled her closer, so that she was half lying on the table on her stomach. He dress was scrunched around her waist, displaying her lower half to the men. Jake got up from the table and made his way over to her. He was the only one of them who hadn't yet seen her in some state of undress.

He ran his fingers over the welts the belt had left. "Poor thing," he said. "What did she do to deserve this?"

"She kept me waiting."

"Let me borrow her for a little while. I'll soften her up for you. She just needs someone to be gentle with her. You're too intimidating. Remember how Trish was at first?"

"No. If you're soft, you just teach her to manipulate."

Veronica gritted her teeth, willing herself not to scream at them for talking about her like she was a lamp or chair or not right there, leaned over the table on display.

Jake still stroked gently over the welts, eliciting a small whimper from her. She winced when he pressed a finger inside her ass.

"We don't have time right now," Luke said. "There's too much work to do. Tonight we'll play with her."

"All of us?"

"Yes."

Jake removed his finger, and Veronica let go of the breath she'd been holding. Then he smacked her over the still-painful welts and pulled her dress down.

She spent the rest of the day fretting over what all of them playing with her meant. Just when she was trying to test what would happen if she didn't fight him, Luke had to go and introduce new things.

Lunch went off without a hitch, the men too wrapped up in the day's chores to mess with her. She waited on them, and brought them their food, and cleared the table when they went back to work. She checked on the garden and made a note to tell Luke about some holes in some of the bell pepper leaves. She'd fed the chickens and done laundry and cleaned the house.

Around five thirty, Luke came in with a package wrapped in white paper—meat from one of his cattle. "It's stew meat," he said, putting it on the bottom shelf of the fridge. "Make shish kabobs for dinner, for all of us on the grill. The skewers are in the top draw on the left side of the stove, and here's the list of the veggies to pick from the garden for them." He passed a piece of paper to her. "The only other thing you need for your part is pineapple, and Robert's gone out to the store to grab one and the other things we need. Don't look so terrified. We're just having a little party tonight."

The little party *turned out to* include party trays, S'mores, a big bonfire, and a lot of alcohol. The more they drank, the more worried she got. The shish kabobs had been a hit, and nothing dirty had happened yet except for the occasional grope, but she could tell they were just getting warmed up. The grill had been brought to the far end of the yard where the bonfire had been started. For S'mores and *ambiance*, Robert had said after his second beer.

Music played on a battery-operated boom box nearby. Bales of hay had been pulled around the fire to sit on, and before the alcohol had flowed too freely, Jake and Luke had brought out a large wooden cross that looked more like a giant X the way it sat, except that it was leaned back a little, not straight up and down. They'd secured it into the ground with stakes. A large pile of rope sat beside it, which gave her flashbacks to the night Luke had taken her. She shook the thoughts out of her head.

Will sat beside her, his hand rubbing her thigh underneath her dress, exciting her in spite of everything. He wasn't bad looking. Nobody here was as rancher-of-the-month hot as Luke, but nobody was a troll, either. "You look scared, honey."

"Of course I'm scared." She was about to be the centerpiece in some kind of orgy. Veronica didn't think straight men routinely liked to get naked in front of each other. It must be why they were packing away so many beers. "I don't like this with alcohol. Luke is already scary enough. I don't need him drunk."

"He can hold his drink. Don't worry. He's not a mean drunk. If anything, as nervous as he makes you, you'll like him this way."

Speaking of the devil, Luke swooped in, then. He pulled Veronica to her feet and swung her around to the music. "I'm tying you up, sweetheart." His tone was light, but still somehow scary.

She didn't quite believe Will's description of drunk-Luke as less intimidating. The only one who wasn't drunk was Will. He must be the designated driver—or the one designated to pull the others off her if they got out of hand. Physically, he was strong; they all were. They had to be for that kind of work, but was he strong enough to protect her if she needed it? And would he?

"Why isn't Will drinking?" she asked, needing to confirm her hope.

"Safety. If you need to be cut out of the ropes for some reason, do you want to trust I haven't had too much to drink to do it without slicing you open?"

At least Luke could hold his drink enough to have that rationale.

"Why aren't *you* drinking?" he asked. "I need you loose and relaxed."

"I don't drink. Not since my freshman year of college." It had taken exactly one year to realize why drunk was only fun the night before.

Wheels were turning in his head, but Veronica had no idea which wheels. Was he going to hold her down and force her to drink out of a funnel? He could make her drink if he wanted her drunk.

"Put your arms over your head like this." He raised his arms to demonstrate, which made him look ridiculous. Yeah, he was a bit silly drunk.

She rolled her eyes but did it, and he pulled her dress over her head. There was a bite in the air that caused her nipples to harden, but the bonfire so close kept the worst of the chill away.

Luke's mouth closed over one of her breasts, sucking on it while Robert watched with a leer on his face.

"We should milk her," he said.

Veronica's eyes widened and she hoped the men were all too drunk to remember any of this in the morning. She looked for Luke's reaction. It was a raised eyebrow.

"She's not pregnant," Luke said.

"It doesn't matter. I saw it on a website. All we have to do is give her hormone shots, and keep trying til we get there. She's already branded, we may as well milk her, too— keep the theme alive."

"You are a freak," Luke said as if he had room to talk with his playroom and video cameras, but the look in his eyes said he thought the idea was just the right level of degrading to be hot. "Have you even tasted breast milk? As an adult?"

"I have," Will said. "When Frieda was pregnant. I got curious."

"And?"

"It's sweet. Not bad. It depends on what you feed her, though. It can taste sour if she eats too much onion and garlic."

"No onions and garlic, then," Luke said as if he were actually considering it.

Will turned red in the firelight.

Luke noticed. "What aren't you telling us?"

Will ducked his head. "After the baby was weaned, I made her keep producing milk for me for a couple of years until she finally got fed up with it."

"What do you think, princess?" He cupped her mound, his fingers slipping inside her. "Survey says, yes. The idea makes our little slut hot."

She flushed and turned away.

"What do you think, Jake?" Luke asked.

"I think it's disgusting. I'm not drinking it."

"More for us, then."

"You know what they call them?" Will asked, too into the idea to let it drop now. "Milk maids."

"Hot," Robert said.

"I still think it's nasty," Jake said.

"And we said you didn't have to participate," Luke said. "Help me tie her up."

Jake put down his beer and followed them to the big wooden X. The two men positioned her on her back, leaning to press against the wood.

"Careful with her brand," Luke said.

"It's not even touching the beam, she's fine."

Veronica's face flamed as they spread her legs wide to tie them down, exposing her more than she'd ever been exposed for any of them. Even in just firelight it was humiliating. Robert and Will watched from a few paces back. Jake helped tie her up, but once she was secured, he stepped back and let Luke go to work.

"This is going to look like a crack-addicted spider's web, with me doing this drunk," Luke said.

"Doing what?" Veronica asked, her curiosity overcoming her fear and embarrassment for a moment.

"Japanese rope bondage. He learned it a few years ago. If he's doing the fancy rope work, you're going to be there for awhile," Robert said.

Robert wasn't kidding. Half an hour later, Luke was just finishing up the knots. He'd wrapped ropes intricately around both of her arms, keeping it as loose as possible around the sunburned areas. On her legs he wasn't so lenient. Then he tied ropes around her upper torso, and her breasts. The constricting nature of that much rope tied with that much time and complexity made her panic.

"Shhhh," Luke said, stroking her hip. "Deep breaths. This is why I wanted you relaxed. Will can cut you out fast if necessary."

"I have a problem," Veronica said, once her breathing was back to normal.

"Yes?"

She flushed and lowered her voice. "I have to pee."

Luke started to laugh.

"I'm serious. I really have to go."

He shrugged, unconcerned with her discomfort. "So pee."

Her eyes widened. "I hope that's a joke. I can't just *pee.*"

Luke's expression darkened. "You can and you will. We are far from finished with you and there's no way I'm undoing all this work so you can take a piss. It's just pee. Do it."

She shook her head and glared at him, her lips set in a firm, defiant line. "I can't." There was no way she could be exposed like that and pee in front of them. It was too degrading and awful.

Robert, who was proving to be the most dangerous instigator of the group, came closer. "This, I have to see."

Within a couple of minutes, all four of them were standing around her, arms crossed, amused looks on their faces—just waiting for it.

"I'm not doing it," she said.

Despite the alcohol that had lightened his mood, Luke's face was stern. "Ronnie, what did we say about you making an effort and seeing how much nicer I could be?"

"I don't care. Be mean, beat the shit out of me, but I'm absolutely not doing it. I'd rather die." She didn't really mean that, she only said it because she didn't think he'd do it, at least not the killing part. He was too giddy with all the perverted things he could make her do to end it all now. The big box of videos he had of Trish said it had been a long time since he'd done all of this, and he wasn't about to end the party now.

"You'll do it. You won't have a choice." Luke turned to one of the guys, "Jake, go get the bong out of the shed."

Veronica jerked her head up at that. They had a bong? When did they have time for recreational drug use? She'd seen the amount of work they had to do, though they did seem to sometimes stop about a half hour before dinner time. Still, she'd never smelled it on any of them.

"You're getting her high?" Jake asked.

"Oh yes."

"Doesn't that defeat the purpose? If she's too stoned to care, it's less fun."

"I'm only relaxing her enough so that she'll let go, not enough to kill the impact on her."

Jake disappeared behind the hay bales and came back ten minutes later with the bong, ready to go. Luke lit it and held the mouthpiece up to her mouth. Veronica preferred to be a little stoned for this, so she chose not to fight him and inhaled.

"Okay, that's plenty, maybe a little too much."

She relaxed. She knew they'd succeeded in their goal when they let out whistles and catcalls. Then she felt the hot, wet stream trickle down her leg.

When she realized what she'd done, the tears started sliding down her face. Luke moved in next to her ear. "Don't let them get to you. They're just fucking with you. They're drunk as hell and won't remember it in the morning."

The small gesture caught her off guard. "What about Will?"

"Well, you know about him and Frieda. He's probably the freakiest fucker here. Nothing fazes him, so don't worry about it."

Robert came up with the water hose and Veronica cringed, afraid he was going to hose her down like some prison movie, but he was only cleaning her off with a light mist.

Luke seemed to have sobered up as he approached with that predatory look in his eyes. Despite the discomfort since he'd tied her to the wooden beams, and despite the other men looking on, her mouth watered when he unzipped his pants. However sober he appeared, he had to still be buzzed if he was casually dropping trough in front of the others.

"Beg me to fuck you, sweetheart. I want the guys to hear how sweet you sound when you beg me."

Veronica's heart beat harder, and the relaxation that had hit her with the marijuana faded as everything came into hyper focus. If she didn't do as he requested, he might beat her and then force her. She needed to feel at least the illusion of consent. It was impossible to fight him with the ropes tied so tightly around her, especially outnumbered as she was.

Her real choice wasn't whether she would consent or not. The real choice was whether she would try to separate herself from the event, try to hover outside her body or if she would connect and feel and accept what these men would do to her. The latter was a terrifying idea that every cell in her body bucked and rebelled against, but the former . . . if she separated she might become so lost she never found herself again.

Veronica closed her eyes and forced the words past her lips. "P-please, Sir, fuck me." When she'd said it, the throbbing need began between her legs.

"In front of my men? You dirty slut. Do you like being watched, Ronnie?"

"I-I don't know."

It wasn't as if the idea of his ranch hands in some kind of circle jerk around her hadn't entered her filthy mind, but she hadn't thought they'd actually act it out. She wasn't sure she could handle the reality when she couldn't control the outcome.

"Do you want to find out?"

She bit her lip and nodded.

Luke looked back at Robert. "What did I tell you? Do you trust my judgment now?"

Robert tossed back another beer. "Sure, boss. I trust everything you say right now."

Luke stepped out of his pants, and Veronica licked her lips. He was hard and ready, but he still lazily stroked his cock, watching her. He finally filled her inch by agonizingly slow inch. He trapped her gaze in his as his hand dug into her brand.

"Ow!"

A slow smile. She wouldn't have guessed a rancher would know anything about the art of subtlety or innuendo, but the pain and grip on her hip hadn't been accidental. When he entered her, he wanted her to remember which one of them she belonged to.

He stroked gently over his mark. "Shhhh," he murmured, trailing wet kisses over her neck. He began to move in a languid pace, dragging out her torment, while his men chanted and egged him on in the background. Mortifyingly she'd gotten wetter when he'd gripped his mark and hurt her, the tinge of masochism coming out to betray her just like her cunt had.

Robert got impatient. "Hurry up. I want my turn."

"You'll get your turn. You might want to stay sober enough to get it up."

"Fuck you, Luke."

He just laughed and continued to piston in and out of her. Veronica had moved past the embarrassment point. The boom box had run out of batteries and died, leaving only the crackling bonfire and the chirping crickets. The night felt unreal and ancient, and when she looked up, the stars seemed to beckon her to join them. It was like the day before when she'd lain in the grass, floating on the endorphin rush from the branding.

Whatever was happening wasn't about doors and misogyny and rights and indignation. It wasn't about which gender made more money or if men objectified women too much in bikini contests. It was pure, raw animal lust that reached inside her and flipped something low in her gut.

He gripped her hip again, jolting her out of the state she was in, dragging a whimper from her throat and her attention back to him.

"Who do you belong to? Whose mark do you bear?"

"You . . . y-yours," she panted.

Then for the second time with him, she came. The men shouted and whistled and catcalled, adding to the surreal nature of the moment. Luke pulled out and finished by hand, leaving a trail of cum dripping down her stomach.

"Next!" He pulled his jeans back on and zipped up, then went to sit on a bale of hay, his dark eyes never leaving her.

Robert stalked her, purpose in his gaze. A tear slid down Veronica's cheek and she closed her eyes. A calloused thumb brushed it away.

"If you don't want me, I won't fuck you, darlin'. I'm not a rapist."

Was Luke? Yes, no, maybe . . . but . . . it hadn't felt that way while he was inside her. She'd chosen to be there for the experience instead of disconnecting, and she felt more high from the rush than the drugs they'd given her.

Had there been a single moment in which she hadn't wanted Luke's hands on her? She'd been afraid he might kill her or hurt her, but afraid he might fuck her? She couldn't remember. She might have protested his ownership of her, but her body had known its master the moment he'd gotten close enough for her to get a whiff of his aftershave.

Veronica's attention snapped back to the naked, erect man in front of her, so strong and muscled and tan, with sun-bleached streaks of blond in his longish hair. Then she remembered he was waiting for some sign of consent.

"Really? Y-you wouldn't just t-take me?" She wasn't sure she believed the nice-guy act. Maybe he was setting her up for punishment.

Would Luke be angry if she refused his friend?

Robert shrugged. "Luke just pays me, and we're friends, but he doesn't own me. I want you though. I *really* want you." He stroked her side, then his fingers drifted down her hip and between her legs.

Neither her mouth nor her body protested when he slid one finger—and then two—inside her, pumping in a slow, easy rhythm. His mouth found the side of her throat and he kissed her softly there.

He whispered in her ear. "If you don't stop me, I'm going for it."

She didn't stop him. But she didn't come, either. Nor had she been as wet as she'd been with Luke.

When Will's turn came, he didn't ask, he just took like he had the right to her because Luke had granted it. She came bucking uncontrollably against him. The same pattern followed with Jake. Though Jake was gentle, making her come against his fingers before he ever penetrated her with anything else, he hadn't asked for permission.

Her eyes went to Luke to find a dark, satisfied smile on his face. Did he know Robert was the only one she hadn't come with? Did Robert know? Was he offended? Was she going to be punished for it?

A look passed between Robert and Luke that she couldn't decipher and didn't know if she wanted to. A manipulation had happened, and Luke had proved his point.

The guys ignored her now, drinking and talking amongst themselves as if she were no longer there as the fire died down.

Veronica's arms and legs were sore from being tied up so long. Luke took a warm, wet wash cloth and washed her, then he untied her. When he was finally finished, her arms went around his neck, too tired and weak to grip very hard, and he helped her back into the house, leaving the others behind.

Neither of them spoke as they went up the stairs. Veronica's head was too full. Even if Robert and Luke had orchestrated it as some sort of fucked-up object lesson, it still troubled her. The men who had taken without waiting for an invitation had made her come. The one who'd shown consideration and asked permission, hadn't.

Her lack of protest after the option had been granted with Robert, had been a tacit consent, but it had amounted to pity sex. The kind she'd had with every *is this where you want me to touch you?* man she'd been with in the city. She hadn't said no to any of the others, including Luke. Perhaps that was a kind of tacit consent as well, but if she'd said no, even if she'd cried and panicked, she couldn't be sure if any of them would have stopped.

No, that was wrong. When she'd had a breakdown in her bedroom the other night over the forced masturbation, he'd stopped and rocked her and comforted her. He'd thought she was Trish at the time, but still, she could reach him. His love for Trish reigned him in. His former lover was now Veronica's guardian angel.

When they arrived at the top of the stairs, she turned toward her room, needing to fall back into a blank sleep so her mind wouldn't be so busy and troubled.

"Veronica."

Her hand was on the doorknob when he said her name.

"Yes, Sir?"

"Come. You're sleeping with me tonight."

She shouldn't have felt a thrill at being invited into his room like it was dinner at the White House, but she couldn't help it. Her body was eager to please him and didn't care what her mind thought about any of it. Being invited into his bed to sleep meant he was pleased with her, and as much as part of her cringed and resisted, another part was his.

Seven

Luke showered while Veronica made breakfast. She was startled when Robert came in the back door. He didn't appear to have a hangover—a seasoned drinker.

She blushed and turned back to the frying pan. "I didn't make enough for you. It's your day off. I t-thought it would only be me and Luke today."

Luke came downstairs then, wrapped in a towel. He arched a brow.

"I don't like the plan," Robert said, aiming his words at the boss. "I don't want to be the good cop. I want her to come for me."

Veronica's breath caught in her throat.

"Let her have breakfast first."

Her hand shook as she put the food on plates and took them to the table. When she went to get the milk from the refrigerator, Robert eyed the glass jug, and a lascivious smirk lit his face. He hadn't forgotten the previous night's conversation.

When she glanced over at Luke, his face betrayed nothing. She could still hope he'd forgotten the milking idea and that Robert wouldn't bring it up. It was too degrading to contemplate. Somehow worse than the branding, even.

"Eat, Ronnie," Luke said.

It was hard to concentrate on her food with Robert leaning against the counter, his arms crossed over his chest, waiting for her to finish so he could have the thing he'd probably lost sleep over, the thing he'd probably jerked off in the shower over. She squeezed her eyes shut and tried not to be aroused over the idea. There was something so wrong with her. She ate more slowly to prolong her unmolested time.

When her plate was clean, Luke said: "Go to the playroom. Take your clothes off, and be in the position for punishment."

Her eyes widened. "B-but I didn't do anything wrong."

"Do what I asked. We'll be up in a minute."

Veronica bit her tongue to keep from arguing with him and took her dishes to the sink while the men discussed ranch stuff that was far outside her expertise. They were still engrossed in their discussion when she ascended the stairs to the playroom.

Fifteen minutes later, the door opened and the men came in. Luke sat on the leather couch, his legs sprawled open in a casual sort of way. Every time he sat like that, she wanted to crawl over to him and perch between his legs, waiting for permission to give him pleasure. She tried to shake that image out of her head and the arousal it brought with it. Robert stood over her, the tension coiled tightly inside him.

"She's all yours. Do whatever you like with her," Luke said from across the room.

She tensed when the edge of a riding crop stroked gently across her bare bottom, followed by a sharp snap against her skin that drew a grunt from her.

"I'm not pleased with you," Robert said.

She wanted to appeal to Luke. Surely he was the only one who had to be pleased with her. After all, it was his initial on her hip. But since he'd given permission, it seemed Robert's displeasure was his by proxy.

"If you didn't want to fuck me, you should have said no. Why allow it to happen and not give me your pleasure? You gave it to the others. You withheld with me. Why?"

She remained quiet, unsure if the question was rhetorical and even less sure she could manage a response that wouldn't just piss him off more.

"Answer him, Ronnie. You need to say it out loud. We both want to hear it." Luke leaned forward, his forearms resting on his knees.

"I couldn't come," she said, her eyes shut.

Robert circled her, allowing the crop to trail along her exposed flesh as he went. She shuddered each time it moved to a sensitive spot: between her legs, over her ass, across the brand. "At least I got to be there when you were marked."

Any hesitation the ranch hand might have felt over helping brand her had dissipated completely to leave behind the horny lech who'd go as far as Luke would allow.

"Tell me why you couldn't come, darlin'." His voice was low and soothing as if he were trying to calm a spooked mare. But that voice didn't fool her, she knew the freak that lay behind it.

She was silent for several seconds until the crop came down hard against her ass.

"You better tell him," Luke said. "He'll switch to the cane if you don't. Have you ever been caned, sweetheart?"

She shook her head against the carpet, holding back tears. "No, Sir."

"I'm told it's extremely painful. The kind of pain that takes your breath away and makes you want to die until it passes. It would be much easier if you answered the question."

The crop came down again—harder than the first time—causing her to cry out and grip the edge of the rug. "P-please don't."

"Answer! Why couldn't you come?" Robert asked again. His voice had gone scarier.

"You didn't make me."

"Is it the only way you can come? If we make you?"

She cringed at his tone, fearful he'd hit her again. "I-I don't know. Maybe."

"Roll onto your back."

Veronica rolled over, her eyes still shut. On her knees with her forehead on the carpet, she'd been able to stay in a space inside herself, in the room but not totally there. On her back, with no way to shield her facial expressions or hide her tears, she felt more exposed before them.

She shivered as the crop gently caressed her face, her neck, down between her breasts, then between her legs.

"Open your eyes, slut."

When she hesitated, the crop came down over her most private area. She shrieked and her eyes shot open.

"That's better. Now come for me."

It was the scene in the bedroom with Luke a few nights ago all over again. Except this time, both of them watched her. She wasn't sure what it was about this that was harder than anything else she'd endured since she'd come to the ranch.

She turned to Luke, her lower lip trembling. "P-please, Sir . . . "

"Why are you appealing to me? He's the one with the crop in his hand."

"But your brand is on my hip. You're the one who owns me. You can stop him."

Luke smirked. "You say it at the most convenient moments." He stood and crossed to the black toy box then turned the dial on the combination and opened it.

"Stand," Luke said, as he rummaged through the box.

She struggled to her feet and when he'd found the items he was looking for, he led her to the metal pole that looked like a stripper pole but sturdier and larger. He pressed her back against it and wrapped ropes around her torso, tying them securely around her so she couldn't get away, but leaving her hands free.

Next he took a long, dark strip of cloth and blindfolded her. "I think you know what's going to happen, Ronnie. You're going to masturbate for us, or you're going to be in a lot of pain. Do you want that?"

"N-no, Sir."

"The choice between pleasure and pain shouldn't be such a hard choice, don't you agree?"

"Yes, Sir."

He pressed a ball gag into her mouth and secured the offending straps around her head. Being blindfolded had been almost a blessing, but being unable to plead with them was a special kind of hell. What if she was really hurt? What if she couldn't beg for mercy? She believed Luke would come to her aid if things went too far . . . if she could communicate with him. She heard his footsteps move back across the floor and the sound of leather creaking as he sat, no doubt watching her with smug satisfaction.

"Finger yourself like a good slut," Robert said, his voice hard and demanding. Gentle Robert was long gone.

Veronica whimpered around the gag, and the crop came down across her thighs causing her to jerk in her bonds. She was surrounded by and immersed in a melting pot of sensations. The soft cloth over her eyes, the wetness of her tears and between her legs, the burning warmth of her skin where the crop had fallen, the scratchy ropes, the cold, hard pole pressed against her back.

"I can switch to the cane if you need more motivation."

"I think she needs a taste of it before she can know why she wants to avoid it," Luke said.

Footsteps receded. The toy box opened then shut with an angry snap.

Veronica tensed. She tried to beg, but words wouldn't form around the small rubber ball in her mouth. There was no way beyond her pathetic, muffled mewls to elicit pity or mercy.

A sharp slice went through the air next to her ear. She would have hit the ground in a panic if not for the ropes holding her in place against the pole. A moment later when the cane sliced the air again, it connected with her upper thigh.

Her breath left her for a minute, taking her ability to scream with it, but the tears came harder, slipping past the barrier of the blindfold. She didn't have to be asked again. Her hand went between her thighs, rubbing herself as if her life might depend on it—she wasn't sure with the cane in the mix. She spread her legs and pressed harder against the pole as she worked her clit.

"Use your other hand, too. I want those fingers in your cunt. I want you to feel how wet you are. I want to hear it."

Robert had moved closer as he spoke. She didn't hesitate at the new demand. She didn't care anymore how it looked or that they were watching her. She finger-fucked herself, moaning around the gag while she feverishly rubbed her clit with the fingers of her other hand. Her hips moved, bucking against her own ministrations.

"That's it," Robert said. She could practically hear the smirk.

His mouth kissed and suckled at her breast while his large hand closed over the other, rubbing and squeezing. "We are going to milk you like the dirty little cow you are." She whimpered as he sucked harder, as if he could somehow cause lactation with just dirty talk.

Veronica jerked when she felt something cold, greased, and metal slide into her ass.

"Relax, and open." It was Luke's voice next to her ear. Robert continued to play with her breasts while Luke gripped her throat with one hand in a proprietary way as he worked the phallus inside her ass. "We're going to be using this hole, too, sweetheart." When she tensed, he said, "I'm just preparing you. It won't be today."

For the first time she was glad for the gag. With only whimpers and stifled moans, she didn't have to come up with useless protests.

Luke gripped her throat tighter, his mouth at her ear. "Come," he snarled.

She orgasmed around her fingers while the two men continued to stimulate her ass and breasts. When she finished, Luke untied her and carried her to the couch. She heard zippers being unzipped and pants hit the floor. She was positioned so that she straddled one of them. She didn't even know whose cock she was on until Luke said, "Ride him until you come again."

Robert helped her raise and lower herself, but finally, growing impatient, he flung her down on the floor and entered her from behind. She whimpered and panted around the gag as another orgasm built. Then Luke ripped the gag off her mouth and shoved his cock past her lips, his hand grabbing her hair, holding her in place as she sucked, half gagging on him.

The second time she came, the tears poured out of her like they would never stop. It was too much sensation to contain and too many confusing emotions. Robert and Luke finished inside her at almost the same moment, as if they'd done this before. They both pulled out, and Luke carried her to the couch, holding her against his chest, petting her hair and rocking her.

"Shhhh," he said. He took the blindfold from her eyes and wiped the tears from her face. After she'd settled, he said, "Go lie down in your room for awhile. I'll come get you a little later. Robert and I have some business to discuss."

Somehow she knew the business was her.

She flushed and looked away from the other man as she crossed the floor and went back to her room. When she'd shut the playroom door, she heard their muffled voices, but as much as she tried, she couldn't hear anything specific.

Finally, she gave up and crossed the hall back into her own room. She stood for a long time in front of the antique mirror, running her fingers over the welts on her thighs and bottom. Then she got under the covers and tried to relax.

"Wake up, Princess."

Veronica scrambled to sit. She couldn't believe she'd dosed off. She'd only meant to rest and recharge, trying not to think about her morning, or the internal struggle that had accompanied it.

Luke sat beside her, stroking her hair back from her face. "Let me look at your welts and check on your brand."

She pulled back the covers, finally past the point of shyness over him seeing her naked. He'd behaved so much as if it were his natural right, that she was beginning to forget it wasn't. She'd almost started to believe that it was—that the permanent mark he'd burned into her hip had caused her to forever forfeit all rights over her own body. It was as if, along with killing nerve endings, the brand had killed a few brain cells, the ones that might be in charge of charming notions like independence and gender equality.

He ran his fingertips over the welts. "Are they sore?"

"A little." But not as much as the brand. He rolled her over to inspect that next.

He pulled a syringe from a bag, and she struggled to get away. He pressed her down, pushing against her back so she couldn't squirm out of his hold.

"W-what is that?" A million horrible possibilities entered her mind. One of them seemed completely insane. Why would he get her hooked on drugs? But then why would he do anything else he'd done? Because he could. He was already living on the wrong side of the sanity tracks.

"Hormones. We talked about this."

No, they hadn't talked about it. He'd talked about it with his snickering band of ranch apes while she'd been hoping it was just the alcohol talking. Apparently not. Once Robert had brought up the idea and Will had given personal experience, it was a done deal. The men must have been discussing hormone shots in the playroom.

"I-I don't like needles."

"Then you won't like this. Be still or I'll tie you down for it."

"P-please Sir, don't . . . " Her voice closed off as if she were afraid to give more than a token protest. Pre-kidnapped Ronnie would be so disappointed.

He lifted her chin and captured her gaze in his. "Be a good girl, Ronnie. It's our day off. I'll take you for some ice cream if you're good for me."

The condescension in his words didn't matter. The prospect of leaving the house was too novel and exciting. Veronica buried her face against the pillow, unable to look at the sharp needle as it came closer to her hip—thankfully the one that wasn't sore already from the brand.

She dug her fingers into the pillow at the sharp burn and sting as he delivered the hormones, the pain warring with the humiliation of what he was preparing her body to do for him.

He stroked her flank when he was finished. "There, now that wasn't too bad, was it?"

"N-no, Sir," she said, afraid of what result any other answer might bring.

He rolled her onto her back then to play with her nipples. He had to know the hormones wouldn't work that fast. It wasn't a magic potion. It seemed more likely it would take weeks or even months, but maybe he was establishing a ritual between them. He pulled on her nipples, rubbing them between his fingers, then he sucked on each one for several minutes while he massaged the sides of her breasts with his large, rough hands. Despite his ultimate purpose in all of this, her hips arched up, begging for attention below her waist.

Luke pulled away. "You're going to give me milk like a good little animal, aren't you?" She closed her eyes against his scrutiny. He stroked the side of her cheek. "I'm going to condition you to want to give me what I want. By the time your body is ready, the idea will arouse you so much, you'll happily let me milk you every day."

Maybe a part of her sick, twisted mind already wanted to. After all, she'd been wet the night before at the party when the topic had first been broached, and she was sure she was wet again now. As if reading her thoughts, his big hand moved between her legs, rubbing against her opening, a broad smile on his face.

"Don't move. I'll be right back."

He returned with a vibrator and shoved it inside her. Then he went back to his goal of training her body to give him milk. As he suckled on her breasts and rubbed and stroked them, the buzz of the vibrator worked its magic and made her come again.

After Luke finished with her, he allowed Veronica to shower and get dressed again. After sex with the two men, she needed to clean up. She picked a sky-blue cotton dress that fell just below her knees and briefly hated herself for wondering if the choice would please him.

When she descended the stairs, Luke was wearing a pair of jeans, cowboy boots—which she'd learned they just called *boots*—a T-shirt, and a cowboy hat—which going with the pattern, he probably just called a hat.

"What about my shoes?" With shoes she could run. She tried not to let the hope show on her face. Although she found herself deeply aroused by the things Luke and the ranch hands did to her, she couldn't stop trying to get away. She didn't know what she'd do once she escaped. She couldn't think that far. If she let herself think that far, she'd have to deal with the hopelessness of her life. The debt, the dwindling bank account, the fear. But Luke could still do anything to her. She needed to remember that.

"You won't need them, it's a drive-up place. We're staying in the truck."

So much for that. She tried not to look too disappointed.

"Come here."

When she came closer, he pulled her onto the couch with him and snapped a metal cuff around her ankle.

"What's this?"

"Insurance," he said.

She wasn't sure what that was supposed to mean, but she didn't think she liked the glint in his eye. He released her then. She'd gotten only a few steps to the door when an electric zap shot up her body. She crumpled to the ground, shrieking so loudly she could barely believe the noise had come from her own mouth. She convulsed a few more times, then lay still, disoriented and terrified.

Yes, Luke could do anything.

He stood over her, a small remote in his hand. "If you try to signal for help in any way, I will push the button, and I won't push it just once." The shock cuff made even the idea of branding seem like child's play.

She cringed when he helped her to her feet. "You didn't have to do that."

"So, you aren't still planning your escape? It's only been a few days. As much as you rant about how you don't need a man, I figured you'd still be plotting and waiting for your opportunity."

Veronica looked at the ground, giving him all the information he needed.

"If I thought I could trust you, I wouldn't need it. I'm not going to prison for rescuing you."

No, he'd go to prison for forced labor, false imprisonment, rape, and battery. The next to the last charge she wasn't sure she believed. In spite of everything, she wanted his hands on her, his cock between her legs—or in her mouth. She didn't want to be caned or whipped or electrocuted or given injections every day, but the rest . . .

They didn't speak on the way to the truck. He opened the door and helped her into the passenger side, and this time she didn't have a smart retort for him about her ability to open her own doors. She was just glad there was a part of him that could be nice to her. When she was strapped in, he slid his hand up her thigh and smiled when he didn't find panties. She still couldn't understand why she'd made that choice today.

"You're learning," he said. He pulled her dress back down and got in on the other side.

During the drive to the ice cream place, she eyed the remote. It peeked out from his shirt pocket, appearing nondescript and innocent.

"When we get back home, are you going to take the cuff off?" She held her breath, waiting for his response, hoping he wouldn't leave it there with the option to electrocute her anytime he wanted.

"Of course. I don't like using it. It's a bit cruel." At least he knew that. At least he had a line in the sand somewhere that he'd prefer not to cross too often. "I just don't want to go to prison. You understand that, don't you, princess?" He brushed a stray hair behind her ear, then turned his focus back to the road.

"Yes, Sir." She didn't dare bring up the point that he wouldn't have to fear prison if he hadn't kidnapped her, and even then he wouldn't have needed to fear it very much if he hadn't ordered her around, prevented her from leaving, and . . . all the rest.

The trees passed by them in a blurred strip of green as they drove down back road after back road. She stared out the window. "You wouldn't have to worry about me trying to escape if I wasn't so afraid of you. I-I mean, I don't hate the ranch completely." She chanced a glance over to find a grin inching up his cheek, but his eyes were on the road. Smug, self-satisfied bastard.

It was hard to hate the ranch with the animals and the garden and open sky, and his nice house and good food. It was hard to hate sexual pleasure. It was hard to hate the little comforts he gifted her with even while he demanded so much from her.

A hand came to rest on her knee, pushing back the edges of the skirt to stroke her leg. "I told you the first week or so would be the hardest. You'll settle in. You've already softened so much toward me. I don't think you realize how much. You don't complain about your chores anymore. When I come near you, you lean into my touch more times than you pull away. And your body is so soft and yielding."

Her face heated at his words. She wanted to yell and fight, but the remote in his pocket made it safer to remain silent. *Pretend that's why, Ronnie.* It was easier to tell herself that the stifling of her rebellion was because she was afraid he'd push the button, or because a man who would brand you like cattle even while you begged him not to might do anything.

His hand moved from her thigh, and then his fingers threaded through hers. He brought the back of her hand to his lips and pressed a kiss to her skin.

"I take care of what's mine, princess."

Somehow the derisive pet name had turned into an actual term of endearment over the course of the past few days. She tried not to respond to his lips against her hand or the words as they rumbled over her, but the fight was pointless. If he'd stopped the truck and taken her in a field somewhere, she'd be up for it. She'd be wet and pliable and yielding. She'd surrender to him out in some wheat field like a rutting animal. Veronica pressed her thighs together, trying to soothe the ache between them.

If he was so sure she was his, he wouldn't have put a shock cuff around her ankle. If he wasn't sure, then maybe she wasn't his yet. Maybe she was still hers.

Fifteen minutes later, they pulled up to an old-fashioned drive-up restaurant that seemed to specialize in ice creams

and milkshakes. A teenaged guy came up to the window as
Luke rolled it down. "I just want a chocolate milkshake. And
what do you want, sweetheart?"

"The same," she said, not wanting to have to pick from
the menu while her heart was fluttering in her chest so hard
it made it difficult to think. Part of it was the sweet way he
spoke to her in front of the teenager, like they were a couple
on a normal Sunday afternoon jaunt. Part of it was over the
introduction of a stranger who might help her if only he
thought she needed it. And then part of it was the fear of
Luke's wrath coming down if she tried anything, angrily
pressing that button until she went unconscious while he
peeled rubber to get out of there.

He squeezed her knee while the guy went to get their
shakes. "You could have had anything off the menu," he
said, still sounding like a boyfriend—doing funny things to
her brain and heart.

"Nobody can screw up a chocolate shake," she said, feeling awkward and weird like she was on a first date. Some
insane part of her brain decided she was. But it wasn't the
kind of first date young girls giggled and daydreamed about.

The guy came back a few minutes later with their
shakes, and Luke paid him then started the truck. She didn't
want to go back to the house yet. Even with the fresh air and
people around her and plenty of chores to keep her busy, she
missed being out.

"Are we going back home now?" Why had she called it
home? If the look on his face could be trusted, Luke had
caught the slip as well.

"Not just yet. I want to show you something first." They
drove for a long time in silence until he pulled onto a dirt
road with a state park sign. They went down the road for a
few more miles until they came upon a large lake.

For an insane minute she thought he was going to drown her. Maybe he worried the boy at the drive-in restaurant had been suspicious, and she'd proven too great a liability. She was about to beg and plead her case when he spoke.

"Don't look so spooked. The weather's about to get too cool for this. No one's around. Let's skinny dip while it's still warm enough to enjoy it. He took a key from his pocket and bent to undo the cuff around her ankle, then he came around to the other side of the truck to let her out, peeling his clothes off along the way.

She tried not to drool over his physique, but every time she looked at him naked or half-naked, something low inside her responded in a primal sort of way she couldn't deny. It was the kind of way that knew nothing of cell phones or television or takeout or society. That part of her wanted things to be simple in the way they weren't in the city. The ranch was hard and at times scary, but it was simple. She'd yet to even see the computer he'd promised to show her. For all she knew it was just a laptop locked up in his safe. It seemed most likely at this point.

Veronica didn't resist when he pulled her dress off and let it fall into the pile of clothing he'd created.

Her teeth chattered when they got into the water. Luke's eyes went straight to her breasts as her nipples became hardened points.

"Give it a minute, you'll get used to it," he said, trailing his fingers over her breasts and moving in to kiss the side of her neck. It seemed to be Luke's mantra about everything. If something was uncomfortable, she'd get used to it. This was the only way the female of the species ever could have survived . . . by getting used to everything.

He swam out a little way, and she followed him. When they were far from the shore, he said, "If you didn't trust me, you would have gone for the shore and the keys in the truck, not followed me out here. Do you know how at my mercy you are right now?"

Her blood ran colder than the water, but she forced herself to hold onto her bravery. "I've been at your mercy since you took me."

"Good answer. Now tell me you trust me."

Veronica balked at the request. Of all the things he could have asked her for—all the dirty and degrading things—it was this thing, this small verbal acknowledgment that she couldn't give him. It felt like losing everything—like selling her soul.

He raised an eyebrow and waited. "I haven't drowned you, yet. We're alone in the middle of nowhere. It would be easy. How long do you think it would take them to find you? From what you told me that first night, nobody would be looking. It could be years. Certainly long enough for that brand to decompose off your body. And then what link would there be to me?"

She started to swim at a feverish pace toward the shore, desperate to get away, to lock him out of his truck and just drive forever.

He easily caught up with her in a few short strokes. It was obvious he swam a lot when he could get away from the ranch. "Tell me."

"Tell me you trust *me*," she countered. He clearly didn't. Men and their double standards.

"That's different. You could send me to prison."

"You could take my life. You just got finished laying it out point by point. The stakes are bigger for me."

He nodded. "All right." He moved them closer to the edge where he could stand, but she couldn't yet. Before she could get much of a breath to hold, he pushed her under.

In the first few seconds, she panicked, thinking he'd finally crossed the last line. Maybe the story he'd just painted sounded safer. Dimly in the back of her mind, she didn't think he'd drown her. She believed he was only screwing with her, trying to scare her and intimidate her into obeying his earlier request. But what if she was wrong? He'd already shown edges of crazy with the episode a few nights ago when he'd called her by the name of his former lover.

In a moment of self-protective madness, Veronica reached between his legs and started stroking his cock. Pleasuring him was the only currency she had to work with. A part of her recoiled at the act, especially under the circumstances as she struggled to hold her breath. His hand loosened on her shoulder and she came up, gasping for air. Then his lips were on hers, his tongue in her mouth.

He pulled away. "Don't stop touching me."

The thought hadn't crossed her mind; she was too desperate to keep him happy so he wouldn't push her under again.

"Take a deep breath," he said.

Veronica shook her head, her eyes widening. "Please, Luke, don't push me under again."

"What did you call me?"

"I'm sorry, Sir." How could she be expected to remember titles when he was scaring her like this?

"Tell me you trust me and mean it."

"I can't."

"Take a deep breath, then."

She wanted to lie to him and give him the words he wanted, but he'd know she was lying. She took a breath and he pushed her under the water again. She stroked his cock with one hand, while she played with his balls with the other, still hoping she was reaching him and he saw the value of keeping her alive, while privately she fantasized about murdering him. This moment was perhaps the most degrading, while he held her life so precariously in his hands and she pleasured him to appease him—to keep breathing.

A few moments later, he came and pulled her back up. She took in gulps of air.

"If I wanted you dead, it would be so simple. Tell me you trust me or we'll do this until the sun sets."

"You can't force someone to trust you!" she shouted. Her survival instinct had fled in the wake of her anger. Let the fucker kill her. What difference did it make at this point? She was his slave. No better than one of his animals. He'd slaughter her the second her continued existence became inconvenient for him. Fuck him and every man on that ranch.

"Then just say the words. Tell me you trust me not to harm you."

Why did he need to hear it so much? Had Trish trusted him? Was it part of the charade of her being his dead lover? If Veronica said it, they could leave, maybe. Despite her anger, despite being at the end of her rope, she didn't want to go under again, and with him spent, she had nothing else to barter with.

"I trust you not to harm me, Sir."

"And eventually, you'll mean it."

She thought he was going to push her under again, but he helped her out of the lake, instead. He took a blanket from the truck and wrapped her up in it until she was dry, then slipped her dress back on over her head and helped her into the truck. He locked the cuff back around her ankle and then put his own clothes back on.

She was crying, trying to wipe the tears away before he could see them when he got back in the truck.

"I didn't hurt you out there." There was the slightest note of regret and guilt in his voice. If he thought he could rationalize now and make her believe it, too . . . he really had lost his mind past the point of return. The thought made her even more afraid.

"You scared the shit out of me," she said, her tone bitter. "I get it. You're all powerful. You can stop lording it over me. You know I'll do whatever you want to stay alive."

He started the truck and eased it down the dirt road. "I want everything, Ronnie. Not just your body. I want your soul, your every thought and desire. I want it all. By the time I'm finished, you'll give it to me."

"Or you'll drown me?"

He pulled the remote out and raised an eyebrow. "I don't want to use this on you."

She shut her mouth and looked down at her hands. If he didn't want to use it, it was a simple matter of just not using it, but she didn't dare give that thought voice.

They drove in silence for a while and he finally said, "You're so like her. Just *be* her, please. Be Trish." His voice cracked.

This time the glimpse of vulnerability didn't make him seem as crazy and unhinged, just sad. So terribly sad. And broken. She wondered if he fully comprehended how wrong his actions were, or if he was just so desperate to bring back a ghost that he couldn't see anything else but Trish. Veronica was a casualty in his quest to work magic to transform her into another woman, and he didn't seem capable of understanding what he was doing.

Sympathy and hate warred within her. She wanted to escape him, but at the same time, it hurt her that when he looked at her, he saw another woman sitting there. What would it be like for him to look at her and see *her?* To want *her* instead of a passing specter? Instead of the phantom that sat in the sixth chair at the table for their morning and afternoon meals.

"Would you have taken me if I didn't look like her?"

"No," he said. There was a conviction in his voice that she couldn't deny. At the very least, he believed it.

The admission only made her more confused. In a sense he *had* rescued her. In her thoughts of escape and freedom, she'd tried not to think about what she'd be going back to. If he hadn't taken her where would she be by now? In a soup kitchen line? Sleeping under a bridge if she didn't make it to the shelter in time, or if they were too full? What about when winter came? The only thing that had put her in a warm bed with food in her belly was her resemblance to Luke's former lover. He couldn't have victimized her other-wise, but he wouldn't have saved her.

They stopped at a four-way stop sign and he turned to her, his eyes so dark and intense she wanted to find a way to hide under the seat or just disappear for a few minutes.

"I'm not kidding, Veronica. You will *be* her. Or else. You'll make me forget you aren't her. I'm not going back to before I found you. You will love me and obey me and submit to me, and you'll do it with that look of adoration Trish used to give me or I'll never stop making you regret wearing her face." His voice had risen as he became more intense. "Am I getting through, here?"

"Y-yes, Sir. I'll be her. I swear. I'll do whatever you want." *Just don't be crazy. Please don't be crazy. I need something safe to hold onto.*

A Sheriff's deputy pulled up at one of the other stop signs and for a moment both Luke and Veronica froze. The wheels spun in her head. If she could get the cop's attention as they passed . . .

"Do it and you might not survive to tell your story. How much of this do you think you can take?" She looked over to see the remote in his hand. The look in his eyes said that whatever brief moments of guilt or regret he felt, he'd do whatever he had to do. "Eyes on me."

Hesitantly, she looked at him. Then Luke stepped on the gas and lurched past the police officer. When they'd passed, she turned in her seat to see the cop go in the opposite direction down the road they'd been on—toward the lake. She wondered if the lake was his destination. Maybe he'd just gotten off work for the day and wanted to fish or swim. What if their timing had been just a little different? What if he'd discovered them in the water?

"Do you think he's going to the lake?" she finally asked.

"I don't know. Maybe."

"What if he'd caught you while I was underwater? Would you have killed me even though it wasn't my fault?"

His only answer was silence. Finally he said, "Going out was a bad idea."

Eight

They didn't speak about the trip again. But when he took her to the playroom that night, the only thing in her head was his demand that she be Trish. She wondered if the afternoon had sobered Luke up, if it had brought home how dangerous the game he was playing with his freedom really was—how easily it could all go wrong. How easily he could be caught. For now, his community thought he was a law-abiding citizen, but how close would he come to unraveling that fiction?

She was finished fighting him. If being his former lover was the only way to stay safe, that's what she'd do. She'd hide in plain sight.

As soon as they arrived home, he disappeared out to the barns, doing God only knew what. Without a list of chores, she went to the living room and pulled out the box of videos. She watched them until he came back inside hours later. When the door clanged in the kitchen, she hurriedly took out the tape and put the box back where it was, darting to the couch to look through a five-year-old magazine on the coffee table.

With the videos, she'd been studying her role. Could she look at Luke with that same look of desperate longing? Could she convincingly fake it? If she'd been the one he'd met first, could it have been real? If things had happened very differently, of course. There was a lot to find appealing in Luke Granger. He was good-looking, hard-working, had his own business, smart, stable—with those isolated psychological exceptions—sexy, kinky. Yes, if she'd been first, she would have looked at him with that helpless devotion. And she would have meant it.

What she had instead was a twisted shadow, and Veronica found herself jealous of a dead woman.

"What are you thinking about?" Luke asked.

"N-nothing, Sir."

She didn't resist when he pulled the dress over her head for the second time that day and took her upstairs to the playroom. When he'd shut the door behind him, he cupped her breasts and stared at them with a mixture of lewdness and anticipation.

"Within a few months, these will have milk." He rubbed his thumb over one of her nipples, causing it to pucker and harden. He bent to drag his tongue over one of the hardened points then suckled at her breast, massaging and kneading like he had when he'd injected her earlier with the hormones. "Tell me you're my cow."

Veronica looked away. It was too demeaning.

"Trish . . . "

"Please don't call me that." It was hard enough pretending. To hear the other woman's name was too hard.

"Trish would have said it. She would have done anything no matter how dirty or degrading just to please me." He wiped the tear off her cheek. "Say it," he whispered.

"I'm your cow, Sir."

"That's right." His hand drifted between her leg and she rubbed her clit against him. He moved closer, his mouth at her ear. "When your body starts doing what it's supposed to do, we'll milk you every day. You'll start to get aroused every time your breasts get heavy with milk. You'll beg me to do it to you like a good little milk maid. And it'll hurt if I don't. I might tie you up and let the pressure just build until you beg to be treated like an animal."

Despite intentionally being called by another woman's name, despite the humiliation of what he'd made her say and what he said to her, his words and touch were getting to her. No matter how wrong, Luke was the only man who could make her feel like she was on fire and cooling off in a stream at the same time.

He backed her against the couch and ordered her to sit and spread her legs. She did as he requested while he moved back over to the video camera to turn it on. Since the early tapes of Trish, he'd upgraded to digital. Her mind raced at all the pornographic websites on the Internet. The sharing possibilities of her sexual disgrace were limitless.

"Rub your cunt for the camera," he said, as he lined up the shot. His words could be as calloused as his hands, but the way he looked at her along with the low growl of his voice made her want him anyway.

She didn't hesitate this time to touch herself, even though he was making a video record of the event. There were already all the videos downstairs. Would someone who watched this one know she was a different woman, or would they just assume they were watching the same girl they'd seen before? If there was already someone who looked so much like her on camera, did this make any difference? She allowed herself to pretend she was the other woman. This could be just another video—one of many and something she got off on.

"I'm going to show this to the guys," he said, and she knew he wasn't bluffing. "Look into the lens and tell them how much you want to give them milk. Will especially is looking forward to it."

Veronica felt the blush travel over her. Not just her neck and face, but her whole body, flushed from humiliation and excitement.

"Say it. I can tell how aroused you are. When they watch this, they'll know, too. They'll know what a filthy whore you are."

She looked at the camera, allowing herself to fall back into the fantasy of being someone else, hiding inside Trish where it was safe. "I want to be your cow. I want you to feed on me."

"Every day," he prompted.

"Yes, every day." She whimpered as she got closer to orgasm.

"Rub those pretty tits for us. You need to prepare them so they'll be ready when it's time. Use both hands, sweetheart."

She didn't want to take her fingers away from her clit when she was so close, but she did what he asked, rubbing and kneading her breasts, pulling at her nipples and squeezing as if she were trying to milk herself. She jumped when a buzzing vibrator was pushed deep inside her, then Luke stepped out of the way so the camera wouldn't miss anything the guys might want to see.

His chuckle was condescending as she worked herself over, drawing a deeper blush from her. "Frieda might want some milk, too. Will you let her drink from you?"

The question caught Veronica off guard, but she was so aroused, that the idea of Will's wife milking her as well sent another surge of lust through her. She wasn't sure if Luke was bluffing or if it might be possible that Will's wife could know about any of this, that she might actually take milk from her breast. But she gave Luke the answer she knew would please him. The one Trish would have given.

"Yes, Sir."

The buzzing stopped and Luke replaced the vibrator with his mouth, lapping at her until she came undone against his tongue.

Later that night, he put her in a chastity belt so she wouldn't touch herself without him. She went to her room, expecting to be invited into his, but waiting for the invitation. *Remembering her place*, as Luke had called it. The words made her cringe at the same time they excited her. They made her angry while they made her want to surrender.

"Goodnight, Princess," he said, going to his own room.

"D-did I do something wrong?" She hated the neediness in her voice. Why should she care if he wanted her to sleep in his room? She could be happy to be left alone, to have her privacy and space.

"What do you mean?"

"I mean . . . c-can't I sleep with you?"

"Not tonight. I need to update the website, and I want you to go to sleep now. Maybe tomorrow."

Veronica lay in bed for what felt like hours while sleep eluded her. She wanted him to want her in his bed overnight no matter how wrong that desire was.

Morning came too soon. Veronica was barely awake when Luke rolled her onto her stomach and the needle slid into her hip.

"Ow!"

His large, rough hand stroked her back. "Shhh, you're okay."

She was still half-asleep when he unlocked and removed the chastity belt. He rolled her back over, immediately going to work on her breasts.

"Finger yourself until you come, slut," he growled in her ear.

That voice. It awakened everything inside her whether she wanted it to or not.

When she'd started touching herself, his mouth latched around one nipple. In the beginning the idea of being milked had sounded disgusting, perverse, even. And definitely demeaning. But the more orgasms she had while he told her how he was going to make her give him milk, and the more attention he paid to her breasts, the more she wanted to give him what he craved.

When she came, he bit down on her nipple. The pain shot a bolt of need straight between her legs, making her come that much harder. He stopped suckling and helped her out of the bed to get ready. He was true to his word about centering all her pleasure around when he was fondling her breasts. She couldn't separate orgasms from that part of her anatomy any more.

Before Luke, she hadn't really liked to have her breasts touched. She didn't get why so many women became aroused by it or why it felt good to them. Her breasts had just been there—pretty to look at, but that was all. Now it seemed they would become almost essential to her pleasure.

As she stood in front of the closet, Veronica said, "Did you milk her?" She was afraid to say Trish's name for fear of how he might react. But they both knew who she was talking about.

"No," he said.

Suddenly the idea was more appealing. It was something different, something that made *her* different. No matter how much he might pretend, he hadn't shared this with Trish. Somewhere deep inside, Veronica hoped it would give her a chance to be seen. For her. The thought troubled her and she pushed it quickly away. If she wanted him to see her and be pleased with her, did that mean she didn't want to escape him anymore? And if she didn't want to escape him anymore, did that make her broken?

Luke left her to go to work while she showered and dressed. Downstairs, she found the list of chores on the kitchen table. This morning's breakfast was big. Ham and eggs and biscuits and gravy. Veronica's stomach flipped as she cooked, worried about how the men would act around her after the party on Saturday.

When breakfast was on the table, she rang the bell and sat down to eat. She was halfway finished by the time they reached the table. The way they leered at her made her wish she hadn't eaten so fast. Soon she'd be out of things to occupy her attention, and she'd be staring at her empty plate.

"Honey, come pour me some milk," Will said.

Veronica looked up, startled to find the men giving her knowing looks. Her eyes shot to Luke, questioning.

He nodded at her. "Do it."

She got up from her chair and took the bottle of milk and poured it into Will's glass. When she bent, she knew the low-cut dress Luke had picked for her showed too much of her cleavage. It laced up in the front, and even though she'd pulled the laces tight before tying them, her breasts nearly spilled out.

When she set the pitcher on the table, Will pulled her onto his lap and untied the laces, causing her dress to gape open and expose her breasts. Her breath deepened as he stared at her erect nipples.

"Soon when I ask for milk, you'll offer me your breast like a good girl, won't you?"

She moaned as he took her nipple into his mouth and sucked, then his hand slid underneath her dress and he stroked between her legs. Veronica squirmed in his lap, aware the others were watching. Jake seemed disinterested —not yet on board with the milking concept.

But Robert just watched her, his gaze intense. "We're glad you're so excited about being our cow," he said. "We all saw the video you made last night."

Will released her breast and she buried her head against his neck. How could they have seen it so fast? They'd been working since early this morning.

"I emailed it last night," Luke said.

When Will finished fondling her, he pushed her off his lap. She kept her eyes down as she started to lace her dress back up.

"No," Luke said. "We want to look at them. You can pretend modesty when we go back to work."

She blushed but left her dress hanging open. Robert grabbed her wrist before she could make it back to her seat. "What about me?"

He unbuckled and unzipped his pants to reveal an impressive erection. "I want to feel your wet little cunt gripping my cock. You got me all worked up squirming in Will's arms that way."

Veronica, looked over at Luke, knowing even before she did it what his response would be. He just raised a brow at her and went back to his breakfast. Well, he wasn't going to forbid it. He hadn't strictly ordered it, either.

Robert backed his chair out and pulled up her dress. "Straddle me. Now." He was almost as frightening as Luke when he got that look in his eyes. But she was glad for it. She hadn't come before Will had been finished with her. Her need was so strong now, she felt as if she was in heat. A thick, demanding cock was more relief than threat.

She whimpered as she sank down on him. He played with her breasts while she rode him. Fucking Luke's ranch hand at the breakfast table while the rest of them continued on with their meals was almost too surreal to accept. But she didn't have much time to think about it before another orgasm ripped through her.

As the last wave of her pleasure crested over her, Robert sucked and bit at her nipples, causing her to shudder violently in his arms.

While he amused himself with her, Will spoke. "I came up with a idea on how to make a milking machine for her. Robert said he can help put it together."

Robert let go of her nipple. "As long as I can still milk her by hand."

"Luke, what do you think?" Will asked.

Veronica wanted to hide her face in Robert's shoulder, but that impulse warred with the need to see Luke's reaction.

"I don't see a problem with that," he said as if it were the most normal thing in the world to talk about.

Nine

The milking machine was finished within three weeks. Once Luke had gotten the idea in his head about milking and drinking from her, he'd been a man possessed. He'd been religious about the hormones and massaging and suckling her breasts, never allowing her to achieve orgasm unless his mouth was latched firmly around one nipple. The guys had created a Frankenstein machine. Part milking and part fucking. It was a frightening-looking contraption that incorporated a bench for her to lie on her stomach. There were places for her breasts to be squeezed for milk, and two penetrating toys that would vibrate and drive into her repeatedly until she nearly went mad from the overwhelming sensations.

The feeling of being squeezed by the machine for milk was painful but also arousing. Without milk, it was going through the motions, but Luke was diligent, convinced that if he was patient, he'd get what he wanted out of her body.

Each night after dinner, Luke put her on the machine for an hour while he dealt with other things like making her list of chores for the following day and any bookkeeping or computer work he needed to do.

Before starting the machine each night, he lubed the parts meant to penetrate her. Then he turned it on a steady speed and left her alone. A strap around her waist secured her to the bench, making escape impossible. The only thing she could do was give in. Two months into this routine, the milk came.

Luke had brought his laptop into the playroom to work from the couch, a coffee pot plugged into the wall and a cup of black coffee in his hand. It had been his pattern for several weeks as if he didn't want to leave her and miss it when it happened.

It started as a tingling and pressure, like pins and needles in her breasts. Between the machine and the vibrators working inside her, it was hard to isolate any one feeling from the whole.

Veronica writhed against the vibrating toys while she watched in fascination as the machine milked her, and the creamy liquid dripped into a glass bottle like the one in the fridge with the cow's milk. Luke unfolded himself from the couch and approached the machine like a big cat stalking prey. He turned it off and smirked at the bottle.

He watched her, sipping his coffee for a while, then he took the bottle off the machine and poured a bit into his cup. She watched helplessly as he raised it to his lips and took a gulp of the coffee with her milk in it. It was humiliating and arousing all at once.

"I normally like it black, but that's good coffee," he said, glee plainly written on his face at his success. "Let's find out if you taste as good from the tap."

She didn't fight him when he helped her off the bench and to the couch. As the time had passed between them, she'd given up the desire for escape. She'd become too addicted to the way Luke and his men touched her and too comfortable with a warm bed, food, and shelter. The weather had turned cold, and these were important things. It was too late for her to have another life, and despite what she was supposed to want, this one satisfied her.

Except on rare occasions when she especially pleased him and he invited her into his bed for the night, she slept in her own room. It had begun to bother her less. He didn't call her Trish now, but sometimes when he called her sweetheart or dear, she wondered which woman he saw. As the time had crept by, it had gotten harder to obsess over the point. The only thing that mattered was the way he made her feel.

He'd been mostly kind—only punishing her when she disobeyed him. The terrifying day at the lake became a dim memory and seemed as if it might have been a dream. He never brought it up again.

Luke's mouth descended on her breast and he suckled. He moaned as the milk began to flow down his throat. If she'd worried he might find the actual taste gross, the worry had been in vain. He drank from each breast until he'd drained her, which didn't take long.

"You'll produce more as time goes on." He kissed the tips of her breasts and cradled her in his arms, then he went back and finished his work. That night, she slept in his room.

The next morning there was no injection. The break in the routine was startling, but not unexpected. Now that she was lactating, it wasn't necessary.

At breakfast, Will said, "I hear you're producing milk like a good cow."

Veronica looked down at her plate, her heart racing, the throb and ache starting between her thighs. Involuntarily, at her arousal, she felt the tingling in her breasts and then the milk as it seeped out and wet her dress.

"Go to him," Luke prompted.

She forced herself to get up from the table and went around to Will. He pulled her onto his lap as soon as she was in easy reach. Since the weather had turned colder, plastic had been put around the porch, and space heaters kept the area somewhat warm. She took her sweater off, and he pushed the thin spaghetti straps of the dress off her shoulders, eliciting a shiver.

A second drop of milk bubbled at the end of one breast and then the other, her body already knowing what was coming and anticipating the release from the bit of milk that had built up in the night.

"Milk them," he said. "The best cow is a cow that can milk herself."

Her face burned at his words, but her hands moved to her breasts to obey his demand. She massaged them and tugged and pulled on the nipples until milk began to come out and dribble down. The ranch hand moved in and licked up the liquid and then latched on to one breast to suck.

"Save some for Robert," Luke said. "She's not producing much yet."

Will forced himself to stop after a few seconds. He looked wistfully at her breasts. "I can't wait until her tits are heavy with the stuff. She'll beg us to drink from her to relieve the pressure. Freida was such a needy little whore when she was producing."

Veronica hadn't been nervous about Will not liking it; he'd drunk from his wife. But Robert only found the idea hot. To her knowledge, he hadn't actually done it. But when he tasted her, he was as pleased with the result as Luke and Will had been.

"She's so fucking sweet," Robert said.

Feeding the men like this made her feel a touch less human—more a thing or animal and less a person. It should have distressed her more, but it was too easy to get lost in the pleasurable sensations, in someone else's satisfaction and happiness.

Jake watched the proceedings with a disgusted look on his face, as if the whole affair were spoiling his breakfast. It filled Veronica with shame, and she wished he'd just leave, but when Robert stroked between her thighs, she was so worked up and well-conditioned that she couldn't stop herself from coming against his fingers. Finally, he released her nipple and held her against his chest, stroking her hair. She was grateful for the comfort.

"Come on," Robert said to Jake.

"No, that's nasty. I don't know what's wrong with you guys. The other kinks are one thing, but . . . this crosses a line."

The ranch hand's judgment cut into Veronica, making her feel dirty. If everyone behaved as if it were okay, it could be okay here. Her world had narrowed to the ranch and nothing else. Her ranch, her sky, her ranch hands. But with the one hold-out, she was reminded how wrong everything that was happening was. It brought back who she'd been in the city. In the city she might have masturbated to an idea this depraved, but she wouldn't have actually done it. Would she? She wanted all of them to drink from her, to make what they were doing feel okay. If even one of them wouldn't conform inside the fantasy bubble, it would only bring reality crashing back in all its stark coldness.

"Just taste her, once," Will persisted. "If you hate it, we won't bother you again."

"Oh, fuck. Fine, bring her over here."

Veronica tensed in his arms as he closed his mouth over her breast and sucked. She expected him to immediately push her away in revulsion after a drop or two had hit his tongue, but he swallowed the milk and kept drinking. His hands tightened around her arms as he gripped her and fed on her.

When he'd had his fill, his mouth moved up to her throat to kiss and suck, and then to her mouth, where he kissed her with a passion he'd never shown with her. Before she could catch her breath, he picked her up and shoved his chair back. He pushed back the plastic flap and carried her to the grass and dropped her there.

For a moment she thought he was disgusted with himself and what he'd just enjoyed. Maybe he wanted to let her freeze. Surely Luke wouldn't let him keep her out there. She wasn't sure what was about to happen until she heard his belt and then the zipper of his pants.

No one stopped him as he shoved her dress up over her hips and entered her from behind. She gasped as he filled her, driving into her in a frenzied state that had her tearing at the frozen grass under her hands for something to hold onto. The stiffness of his erection left no doubt to how much he'd enjoyed feeding on her, and that he'd do it again soon.

When he finished with her, he got up and went back to the table. Veronica pulled her dress down and rolled over, looking up at the sky. The ground underneath her back was cool and the air was chilly. The sky hadn't quite turned that endless gray yet. Despite the cold, it still had a sharp jolt of bright blue. There were no clouds.

"Veronica, come back inside. You'll catch your death out there with no shoes on," Luke said. The plastic around the porch muffled his voice, making him seem too far away to reach her.

She stayed where she was, pretending she hadn't heard him, looking up at vast expanse of sky. Of course he wasn't going to give her shoes—even now. Since it had turned cold, she'd been cooped up inside, the leftover outside chores she would have had falling to Will.

Luke still didn't trust her. He was never going to trust her not to run. She jumped when footsteps pounded toward her, then Luke bent and scooped her up to carry her back onto the porch where it was warmer. He put her back in her chair and went to his seat.

"Didn't you hear me yell at you to come inside? You'll freeze out there."

Veronica shrugged, still feeling surly about the shoes.

"What is it?" he asked.

"I want shoes. I've been here for months. Don't you trust me not to run away?"

Luke went back to his breakfast, ignoring the demand and the question. "I've decided to make a change around here. From now on, you'll address the guys with respect. No first names. I only want to hear 'Yes, Sir' and 'No, Sir' out of you. Is that clear?"

"Yes, Sir," she mumbled. It was ridiculous and the wrong thing to focus on, but she felt as if she were being cast off. If everybody got the same title, was he saying she wasn't really just his anymore? The brand had finally healed to the point where it wasn't sore anymore. She wondered if even his brand meant anything between them, if everyone was to be called *Sir* at the ranch.

"Yes, Master," he corrected.

Veronica looked up suddenly, her eyes going wide. "I'm sorry, what?"

"You heard me. Say it."

She looked around the table at the ranch hands. They watched her, waiting to hear her say the degrading phrase. In all of the videos, Trish had called Luke, *Sir*. To Veronica's knowledge none of the other ranch hands had gotten titles. Veronica had been his slave for months, what was verbal acknowledgment in the face of everything else? Still, an old part of her—from when she'd lived in the city—rebelled against the idea. Accepting she was his slave was a different thing from being his slave. Somehow the former was worse than the latter.

Calling him *Sir* had been difficult at first, but it was no different than a waitress or somebody working customer service. It hadn't been too demeaning to force herself to say, even though it had been hard to get used to.

Luke stood and unbuckled his belt. The leather zipped through the loops so loudly it pulled Veronica out of her hesitation.

They were only words.

"Y-yes, M-master." She'd rather say the demeaning thing than have him throw her down on the ground and beat her in front of the ranch hands.

Luke nodded and sat back down. He folded the belt and put it on the table, as if he wanted to have it ready should he need to call it into action.

Several days passed, and Veronica was finally overcome by curiosity to taste her own milk. Luke caught her and whipped her for it, then lectured her for a good half hour about the evils of drinking or even tasting what belonged to him and his men. Despite the humiliation, she'd become aroused by his irrational demands.

As the weeks passed and her milk began to flow better, Luke changed her wardrobe. One Sunday, when the guys were off, he put her in jeans and a cupless corset to better support her heavy breasts. He circled her in the playroom, sizing her up.

"Since you're our cow, I can't have you covering those lovely tits up. We want to see them all the time. And we want easy access to your milk."

In some way, it was a relief. Without fabric to cover them, they wouldn't chafe. It had begun to be uncomfortable with milk-dampened fabric covering her breasts. Luke had begun to rub some of her milk into her nipples after each feeding—it helped some, but as long as she stayed inside where it was warm, freeing her breasts to the air would help more.

Veronica sucked in a breath as he cupped her breasts in his hands, no doubt feeling the heavy weight, knowing how engorged they were. She was desperate to have him drink from her. Titles were nothing now. She'd do or say anything to get him to release the pressure. Now that her body had finally responded to his training and the hormones, Luke wouldn't allow her to squeeze any of the milk out herself. It had to be one of the guys or he'd punish her. After she'd tried to taste her milk, he'd installed cameras around the house so he'd catch her if she disobeyed.

Even after the cameras, she'd disobeyed once. She'd been too desperate to ease the ache. Her body had gotten used to a feeding schedule, and the men had worked later that evening than usual. Luke had easily convinced her that heavy pressure in her breasts was preferable to the searing pain of the cane.

"Please, Master . . . " Veronica rubbed her breasts against him.

"So eager to give milk," he said, swiping his tongue over one nipple, causing a drop of milk to drip from the other as if it were jealous. "I like that. Between the brand and this, you're hardly recognizable from when I first took you."

She moaned and arched toward him, too distracted from the physical discomfort to contemplate his words. "Please, please please. It hurts, please." Tears slid down her face.

"Not just yet." He wiped her cheeks with the pads of his thumbs. "You've been such a good girl the past few weeks. So compliant and docile. I'm so pleased with you. Do you know how happy you make me, princess?"

He'd let her sleep in his room every night since she'd started giving milk. What he was doing should have upset her more, but it made her feel intimately connected to him, more dependent on him, more addicted to the myriad forms of release he could now offer her.

Release from the busy, loud city and the cramped feeling the place had always engendered. Release from her debt. Release from her fear of starving to death. And the physical releases he offered her when he fucked and fed from her.

She jumped when the door opened and Will walked in, followed by an attractive, slim redhead in her early forties. The woman was dressed smartly in a black suit. She crossed the floor and sat on the couch, crossing her long, elegant legs.

"Good, you're here," Luke said. "Ronnie, this is Frieda."

Veronica's mouth dropped open. Will's wife. Here. She looked away from the woman, afraid she might see the guilt. Not that it had been Veronica's fault. Still, the wife of Luke's ranch hand might not see it that way.

Veronica tried to cover her exposed breasts, but Luke pulled her arms down to her sides and shook his head.

"Can I get you some coffee?" he asked the other woman.

"Coffee would be nice, thank you."

Luke crossed the playroom to pour her a cup. "Do you take it black?"

Freida gave Veronica a long, measured look, her eyes flicking to her breasts in a way that made Veronica blush. "You know I take milk."

He smirked. Luke came back to Veronica and squeezed her nipple over the cup of coffee. She couldn't help the sigh of relief that came with the slight ease of pressure. He passed the cup to the woman, and without turning around, he said, "Veronica, take off your pants."

Veronica froze for a second, still trying to catch her brain up to the fact that Will's wife was here and didn't seem freaked out by any of this.

"Ronnie, do you want to be punished in front of company?"

"N-no, Master." She looked at the rug, her face flaming at having to call him that in front of a stranger, but she was too afraid to leave the title off. She eased the jeans down over her hips and stepped out of them.

She was caught by surprise when Will came up behind her, his hands moving around to her breasts, massaging them but not doing enough to make the milk flow. Even though his hand hadn't strayed between her legs, the arousal was high enough that a little liquid dribbled out of her breasts.

Veronica gasped when Will pushed her to her hands and knees and took her panties down. Freida's expression remained stoic as she drank her coffee and studied Veronica.

She still couldn't believe Will's wife wasn't angry. For months when Will had taken her or drunk from her, she'd thought of his wife and what she would feel if she knew what he was doing with another, probably younger woman. From the looks of things, Freida had known the whole time.

Luke and Freida talked on the couch while Will fucked her.

"How long are you going to make her give milk?" Freida asked.

"As long as I can. A few years for sure, but probably until her body won't let her do it anymore."

Veronica felt a surge of lust at his words. It hadn't occurred to her that he might use her for milk for so long. The idea should have disturbed or repulsed her. Instead, it, combined with Will inside her, had her climbing frantically to orgasm.

Luke may have felt that the branding would make her truly feel she was his and accept it, but the branding had only been the first step. It was being fed from that had pushed her over the edge where the only thing that mattered anymore was having the relief that only Luke or one of his ranch hand's mouths could give her.

"The poor dear," Freida said. "But then, she won't be as uncomfortable here. I had to work outside the home during all that. It was finally too much to deal with. I imagine her life is different."

"Quite," Luke said.

Veronica came, panting and moaning, unable to be quiet even with the man's wife sitting right there. When Will pulled out of her, she dropped to her stomach on the rug and just lay there, breathing, as Luke and Freida's conversation faded into a low hum of white noise.

Several moments later, shiny black boots were next to her face. Sometimes Luke wore them with black pants in the playroom. They were the same boots from the videos. He never wore them out of the house. Out of the house it was always his standard cowboy boots and jeans.

"Are you spent, sweetheart? Because if this is all too much for you, we can just let you go take a nap," he said.

"No, Master, please."

He knew what she needed, he was only tormenting her. If she went to sleep now, it might be another full day before someone sucked the milk out of her. She wasn't sure she could sleep through the pain. She had to have relief now. She'd do anything if it would end in being milked. She didn't even need a mouth. If he'd just put her on the machine she'd be happy. She didn't care if Freida watched. Let her watch. The other woman had been Will's cow. This wasn't new territory in her world.

"I don't know, I think maybe you should go on to bed," Luke said, his tone amused.

She scooted her body closer to him and kissed his boots. "Please, Master," she whimpered. "I need to be milked. Please. You know I can't sleep like this."

"Lick, and I'll think about it."

He was showboating for the other woman on the couch, which made Veronica wonder if Luke had been with her. Well, weren't they all a bunch of deviant swingers? But she didn't care; the only thing that mattered was getting what she needed. She ran her tongue over the boot and up the side.

Luke chuckled. "When I met you that day at the diner and you were so rude to me for simply holding a door open for you, who would have thought you'd be a little bootlicking slut by the time I was finished with you?"

The question was rhetorical, of course. But instead of creating rage, it made her more aroused. How could she be so hot from being treated this way?

"Master, please. Just put me on the machine . . . anything."

"I bet you'd like for Freida and Will to watch you get fucked and milked on that machine, wouldn't you?"

"Yes, Master." She wasn't sure anymore if she was lying, or if she'd merely been given permission to start telling the truth.

"No, I think you've been a good enough slut to get the real thing. Crawl over to Freida and ask her to drink from you."

Veronica's face flamed, but she did what she was told and crawled over to the woman still perched elegantly on the couch with her cup of coffee cooling.

"And, Veronica?"

She turned. "Yes, Master?"

"You will address her as Ma'am."

"Can I give you some milk, Ma'am?" Veronica asked, knowing the desperation must be coming out in her voice.

Freida laughed. "She's a slutty little milk cow, isn't she?"

"She is," Luke agreed.

Veronica caught Luke's eyes, and for a moment she thought perhaps he saw her for her. Was she still Trish when he looked at her, or had this new direction in their relation-ship taken them somewhere where he could see her and want *her* even if it was all wrong and fucked up?

"Come here, dear, let me ease some of that awful pres-sure," the woman said.

Freida's mouth descended on Veronica's breast, and she let out a whimper of pleasure as the woman began to suckle. A moment later, her husband had joined her, his mouth closing around Veronica's other nipple and pulling the milk from her so hard it almost made her dizzy with relief.

Then another mouth was on her—Luke's—between her legs, sucking on her clit. So many mouths on her sucking, hands caressing. Moans of pleasure from her and from the two people at her breasts filled the room.

When the couple had taken all they wanted, they passed her back to Luke.

"She tastes wonderful. What are you feeding her?"

"Mostly what we grow or kill. I don't let her have a lot of junk. And we keep her mostly away from onions and garlic."

"You can tell," Freida said.

When Luke finished drinking, he picked Veronica up and carried her over to the machine. "You've been so good today, let's make sure we drain all the milk out so you can sleep more comfortably."

On the one hand, he was rewarding her. On the other, he also wanted to display and humiliate her some more, and her body had forgotten how to be outraged about it. She didn't resist when he strapped her into the machine. He only had to apply lube to the anal toy. Her pussy was so wet it wasn't necessary for the other toy. He inserted the vibrating rods inside her and turned the machine on.

After that, she forgot about her audience. The sensation of being completely drained of milk while her cunt and ass were being filled was all-consuming. By the time Luke turned the machine off, she'd had another three orgasms. Sleep would be great tonight.

She was only vaguely aware of Will and Freida as they stood to leave. Long, feminine nails skimmed lightly down her back and over her ass.

Freida bent to whisper in her ear. "You were very good, dear. I haven't seen Luke this happy in a long time. You're good for him." Then they left.

She wondered if the other woman thought Veronica had come here freely. She doubted Freida knew the true circumstances of her presence at the ranch. Did it matter anymore?

That night, Veronica slept peacefully in Luke's arms.

Ten

Veronica carried a load of laundry up the stairs late one afternoon. She usually folded it in the playroom because there was so much space on the floor to stack everything. It would have been better to take the laundry up in two trips, but she'd piled it all in the basket to make less work. She'd almost reached the top when her foot slipped, and she fell.

She let out a howl of pain as she struggled to stand. The laundry had gone everywhere, but she didn't care about that. Tears stung her eyes. She couldn't put any weight on her foot without screaming. *It's broken.* The panicky thought rose inside of her. It could be twisted or sprained or just bruised, but deep inside she knew.

What would happen when Luke found out? He obviously didn't trust her enough to give her shoes. He hadn't taken her out of the house since that one day with the ice cream and the lake—the day she'd tried to blot out of her memory because it had scared her so badly. If she could just erase that day, she could make peace with being here.

Ironically, the one thing Luke had done to try to force her trust had eroded it.

He couldn't take her to the hospital. It was too big of a risk. They would separate them in the emergency room and she'd have a way out. He couldn't threaten her with the cuff because if they found it on her, he was done. And the brand on her hip was all the evidence anybody would need. Even if he just dropped her off at the hospital and left, and she didn't know how to get to his house . . . even if she hadn't known his full name, that brand was registered with the state. It would lead the police back to him.

Would he kill her? She hadn't been afraid for her life in months, but now . . . What did you do with a lame horse? Wasn't that the kind of attitude Luke had been raised with? Didn't he see her as just another one of his animals now? They'd had a good run, and now he'd have to take her out back and shoot her?

The rational side of her said that was ridiculous. Luke would never do that. But would she have believed before she came here that he would have done any of the rest? When she'd sat in the diner with her coworker, watching him put away that giant breakfast?

The day leaving the lake, he hadn't answered about what if the cop had found him. If she'd been under the water, there was a good chance Luke would have kept her there to save his hide. He'd been adamant about not going to prison, which seemed funny for a man so comfortable with doing crime.

Maybe it wasn't broken. Or maybe it would heal okay on its own. She didn't have to do outdoor chores right now, just stuff inside. Nobody saw her except at meal times and Luke in the evenings. Maybe she could cover it long enough to heal a little. Then she could plead her case. If it was broken it could heal wrong and always hurt, or make her walk wrong or look strange, but at least she'd be alive. Assuming Luke didn't find her repulsive after that.

Veronica scrubbed the tears off her face. Ice. Whatever it was, ice might help. She crawled to the kitchen, unable to put even the smallest amount of weight on it without agony and pulled herself up on one foot next to the freezer to make an ice pack. Her foot was swelling fast. There was no way she'd be able to keep it a secret for long.

He'd know tonight. Even so, she couldn't stop herself from trying to hide all evidence that anything was wrong. After she'd iced it, she crawled back to the laundry to get it out of sight. Thankfully she didn't have to worry about dinner tonight. Chili had been going in the crock pot since after breakfast.

She made it to the couch and covered her legs with a blanket and read the five-year-old magazine Luke wouldn't toss.

The kitchen door clanged shut an hour later.

"Why isn't the table set?"

"I-I'm sorry, Master."

"Well, get in here." He stood in the doorway watching her, an irritated look on his face that she'd keep him waiting when he'd been out working so hard all day.

He watched her as she struggled to stand. She tried to mask it, thinking she could force herself to step on the foot just a little, and he wouldn't notice. But when she tried, the pain shot through her sending her to the floor.

"What the hell happened?"

She cringed at his tone, and scooted away. "I hurt my foot. It's nothing, really. I'm fine. It's okay. I'll be okay."

"Let me see it," he demanded.

Veronica cried harder as she showed him. It was silly to think he wouldn't have noticed—even if she'd tried to walk normally and succeeded. It was too swollen.

He let out a low whistle when he saw the damage. "I'm going to get you changed and take you out to the truck."

"Please don't kill me," she blurted out, the panic edging out her pain. "I'm yours. Please. It'll heal. I'll get better." She'd started shaking and couldn't get the tremors to stop.

"For God's sake. Why would I kill you?"

"Well . . . I k-know you can't take me to the hospital . . . "

"Like hell I can't. Where else did you think I'd take you?"

Veronica wisely shut her mouth. If the thought hadn't occurred to him how close her freedom and his imprisonment were, she wasn't going to remind him of the risks.

"I told you I'd never kill anything that looks like her. Never hurt anything that looks like her. Did you not hear me when I said that? God dammit, do you think I'm a liar?" His voice rose as he spoke.

"N-no, Master. I'm sorry."

He carried her upstairs and changed her out of the corset and into a sweater, then he carried her to the truck.

The drive was quiet, and a part of her wondered if he was telling the truth about the hospital. Surely he had to know this could end badly for him. Why would he put himself at risk?

As if he'd read her mind, he said, "You're not going to tell them anything. I know what you need, Veronica. I may not have done it in a legal or moral way, but I gave you work to do and a safe place to live and food and clothes. You're happy with me. You know you are. I took you away from that shitty life you had. And I know how much you want me, how much you crave what we do. Your body tells me, and sometimes your eyes do, too. Think about all that when they take you back. Think about the fact that I haven't damaged you, or done anything you haven't ultimately gotten off on. Think about the life you'd have to go back to if you turned me in. I know you aren't going to do it. What reason besides silly pride would you have to throw your life away?"

There was no fear in his voice when he said it. He wasn't trying to convince himself, he was already convinced. He truly believed she had a better life as his slave than she'd had in New York, where she'd only been a slave of a different type. In the city she'd been a slave of the impersonal debt hanging over her head and her job with the lack of people to reach out to for help. But despite his conviction, there were still things that didn't match the words he spoke.

"If you believe that, why don't I have shoes? It's winter."

He shrugged. "I like you that way. Vulnerable. Sexy. It's just because I like it. I didn't think you'd run. I haven't thought that for a while."

"But you haven't taken me out, not since that day . . . "

"God dammit, Veronica, do you WANT me to kill you?"

"N-no, Master."

"Then stop arguing against yourself and be grateful I'm taking you to a doctor instead of putting a bullet in your head. Fuck."

His knuckles were white against the steering wheel as he drove. When they passed the road that led to the lake, his gaze went that way, as if for one fleeting moment he considered taking her back and drowning her. Veronica held her breath, silently praying he wouldn't make that choice. Then he turned and went the other direction into town, and she released the air.

When they reached the hospital, Luke carried her to an empty corner and sat her down on a padded bench where she could keep her foot up. When he went to the front to sign in, the receptionist shoved a bunch of papers in his face attached to a clipboard.

Veronica sat quietly next to him while he filled out the paperwork. Under name, he wrote: *Patricia Walker.*

Once again she wondered at his sanity and how firm his grasp on reality was. How safe could she be with a man who didn't really know who she was? Or couldn't stop forgetting?

"Luke?" she whispered, afraid she'd get in trouble for calling him by his first name, but knowing realistically she was safe here with so many witnesses around.

He looked up. "Hmmm?"

She pointed at the name on the forms, unsure how to phrase her question in a safe way. Thankfully, she didn't have to.

His voice was low when he spoke. "Part of the benefit to you in being kidnapped is that you no longer have to worry about your debt. You want to change that now with a paper trail?"

He was protecting her.

"But . . . it's insurance fraud." Like such a thought should matter to him in the face of kidnapping.

"I'm paying cash."

"Oh."

She looked down at her hands while he finished filling out the forms, occasionally asking her questions such as allergies that could put her in harm's way if incorrect. Wouldn't they know Trish was dead? Even if she looked enough like her and even if most of the people here weren't on a first name basis with Luke and Trish, wouldn't it come out that he was giving a dead woman's information?

They had to wait an hour before someone took her back. He held her and stroked her hair the whole time.

Alone in the hospital room, Veronica thought again about escape. She could leave now, easily. Anyone would believe her if she showed them the brand on her hip. Even if the cattle brand had been consensual, it would have been hard, if not impossible, to convince a normal person of that. She was home free if she wanted it.

But Luke was right, where would she go? She couldn't go back to the city where she could barely see the sky for all the buildings and crowds of people. It was too stifling. There was no space there. Everyone was shoehorned in too tight. Human beings needed space. It was hard to breathe there for all the people, all the noise and stress. She needed to see the sky to feel right.

And her body had needs now that even with fantasies she couldn't have foreseen. Sure, if she was free, her milk would dry up eventually, but did she want it to? The feeling of Luke drinking from her was exquisite. Beyond just basic survival, how would she go back to how she'd been? The answer was obvious. That door was closed. She couldn't go back. She'd changed too much. He'd softened all her edges so much that the real world would just snag and cut her.

Before she'd always seen herself as strong and independent. But how independent could someone who couldn't control their spending be? Had she spent out of loneliness? Unhappiness? She didn't know, but since coming to the ranch she'd been free of it all. There had been no creditors calling, no bills or shopping urges. She'd been too busy with her list of chores to think about the mall.

Serving him and his men domestically and sexually should have broken her beyond repair, but in a weird way it had fixed what had already been broken a long time ago. Yet, sitting in the hospital room, surrounded by the normal people in the normal world, she was reminded of how wrong this all was. She'd been living in a haze, but in the hospital, the fog felt like it had lifted for a moment. Shouldn't Luke pay for this?

On the balance sheet, he came out ahead with all he'd given her, but something inside her screamed that he must pay.

A nurse came in, then. "Sorry to keep you waiting, Ms. Walker. The man who brought you in, is that your husband? Boyfriend?"

Master. Owner. World.

"Boyfriend," she lied. After all, she wore no ring. It was the most believable of the options presented. It was telling that brother or friend hadn't been among the assumptions made.

The nurse wrote something down on a clipboard. "I'm sorry to have to ask this, but when a woman comes in with a man, injured like this, we have to. Has he hurt you?"

"No!" The word flew forcefully out of her mouth before she could stop to consider her answer. Luke was tall and strong. With the work he did he was *so* strong. Once the immediate fears had died, he was a place of safety she could hide in. Giving him up suddenly felt like opening the door for the tiger to eat her.

Thoughts of ending up starving, giving blow jobs in alleys to barely scrape by, perhaps finding fetishists to sell her milk to, had her quickly defending her captor.

"Are you sure? Because, if he's hurt you in any way, we can protect you. We can get you to a safe house, and you can press charges. I know it might feel like life is over, but it's not. You can start again. People can help you."

She'd already started again. Luke was her do-over. Anything else was just moving backward.

Did her face show her inner conflict? It must if the nurse was pushing on what was supposedly a routine question. Had someone observed them in the waiting room? Had they seen timidity or fear on Veronica's face? Had they seen her pull back from him when she was afraid he might become unhinged over the question about the name he'd written down? What other clues might they have seen? How much had her face given away? How much was it giving away now?

"I'm sorry, but this seems more than routine."

"I apologize ma'am. I usually have an instinct for these things. I could, of course, be wrong."

Veronica became angry. "Hell yes, you're wrong. Luke hasn't hurt me. You don't know what he saved me from. He takes care of me. We're paying good money at this hospital to be insulted this way."

The nurse looked flustered and ducked her head. "I-I apologize. The doctor will be in to have a look at you in a few minutes."

"Thank you."

The nurse excused herself, and Veronica tried to calm down, to stop the trembling that had started in her hands again. All the adrenaline and fear of the day was catching up to her.

Within a few hours she'd been X-rayed and poked and prodded. Her initial gut reaction had been right. She'd broken a couple of bones in her foot. Thankfully, the breaks were clean and they were able to put her in a boot and gave her some crutches with instructions to come back in six weeks so they could check how she was healing.

When Veronica returned to Luke, he didn't appear relieved or uncertain. He hadn't doubted her for a moment. He knew she was his. If anything, the look on his face was smug and a touch arrogant. She wished that look didn't make her so wet.

He wrote a check at the billing desk and helped her back into the truck. She hadn't taken the out she'd been given, but in six weeks she'd have another opportunity. Deep down she knew she wouldn't take that opportunity, either.

They'd been in the truck for about ten minutes when she finally worked up the nerve to ask the question that had been on her mind since he'd first filled out the forms in the waiting room. "Why would you fill out those forms with the name of a dead woman? Why didn't anyone notice?"

She'd expected somebody to at least say something.

Luke let out a long sigh. "Because nobody knows she's dead."

Veronica felt the cab of the truck getting smaller, the oxygen seeping out, leaving her in a vacuum. She felt like that first night when he'd kidnapped her, riding in the truck, feeling like death or torture was only hours away.

She cringed when he reached across the seat and touched her knee. "I didn't kill her, Ronnie. She'd wanted to do a home birth. She hadn't even wanted a midwife. She had a fear of doctors and hospitals, wanted nothing to do with them. She said women had been giving birth for thousands of years without hospitals or specialized doctors. She read all about it and thought she could do it herself. I should have insisted. I was out herding cattle when she went into labor. It came on quick. The baby didn't make it, and she bled to death."

"If you didn't do anything wrong, why does nobody know?" Veronica knew the question could cost her life. If he'd really killed Trish and had some kind of meltdown confession, surely it wouldn't end well for her.

"I panicked. We didn't go into town a lot, anyway. There were no medical records for her with the pregnancy. It just didn't look right. The guys thought I'd be implicated because I didn't get her to the hospital and hadn't made her go for the checkups, like I'd been negligent. And I was, but she begged me not to make her go. She was distraught. On top of that, someone might just think I killed her. Ronnie, there was so much blood. She'd tried to make it out of the house . . . and there was just so much blood. There would have been a lot of questions. The guys helped me bury her and the baby."

He'd gotten choked up, and his hands shook on the steering wheel.

Veronica's heart beat so hard in her chest she could barely hear his words. Should she believe him? She couldn't decide if his story was credible. He sounded sincere, but if he was some kind of girlfriend-killing sociopath, he'd sound sincere and make her believe it. Had Trish ever had an accident that the hospital staff was concerned about? Had people in town thought she was being abused? Had she been?

In the months he'd had Veronica, he'd never been violent. Yeah, he'd punished her in the playroom a few times and spanked her a few times, but it had always been controlled. Not like a killer or abusive boyfriend. Not like you saw on TV or in the movies. He'd never shown a particularly sadistic streak. He was more interested in sharing her and humiliating her than physically hurting her.

"I didn't kill her," he insisted. "How could you even think that? I *loved* her."

Veronica stared out the window, not sure if she could look at him at the moment. "Did you make her fuck your ranch hands? Is that love to you? Do you even know what the word means?"

"That was her idea. The brand, the ranch hands. We had our rough patches trying to make it work, but nearly every kinky thing we did had been her idea."

But it hadn't been Veronica's. He'd been so single-minded in trying to bring back his former lover that he'd taken a darker turn where her consent had meant nothing, because somewhere in his head, she *was* Trish, and Trish had given consent.

"I can't be her." Not only was it a physical impossibility, it hurt too much to be nothing more than a replacement. Like a Trish-shaped blow-up doll.

"I know."

When they got back to the house, he carried her upstairs to bed. She'd expected to be in her room, but he set her up in his, instead, and brought a TV up to keep her entertained. They didn't talk anymore about Trish that day. He made Veronica dinner and drank from her without her having to beg for it.

Weeks passed and she slowly began to hobble around. Luke had hired the services of a housekeeper to take over Veronica's work and cook the meals while she recovered. During those weeks, he kept the playroom door locked.

She didn't know what the housekeeper knew about her—probably nothing if the playroom door was locked. The woman could be an ally if she wanted out, but each day she bypassed each opportunity for rescue. Who would take care of her while she recovered? Where would she go? How would she live?

By the time the six-week checkup rolled around, Veronica had given up the fake excuses. She didn't believe Luke had hurt Trish, and though she still felt confused about all the things that had happened between them, she wanted to stay. The break in their dynamic from her injury gave her a chance to see her master as just a person. A person who brought her evening meal to her and helped her bathe, and helped her when she made her first few trips down the stairs. A person who seemed concerned for her well-being.

At the checkup, she didn't turn him in. She didn't show them the brand on her hip. She didn't do anything but discuss her foot and go back to the ranch. Soon, as she was able to take on her chores again, the housekeeper was released from her duties, Veronica's last chance to escape drifting out the door with the matronly woman.

Slowly things went back to normal. He had her measured for new clothing, dresses that supported her breasts but left them exposed for his access. The dresses made her look like a serving wench or like what she imagined a *Milk Maid* would look like—according to Will's definition. And he'd gotten her more corsets and jeans.

One Sunday afternoon after her foot had healed and she was walking normally again, Freida came over and took her to the playroom. Veronica thought something illicit was about to happen, but she had a box of hair dye and a comb and scissors and a smock. Nothing kinky.

"It's okay, hun. I do this for a living," the woman said, gently pushing her into a chair.

Veronica could only assume Luke had ordered this. But why? The woman worked quietly. Veronica couldn't think of anything to say to her, and for her part, the hairdresser didn't seem compelled to engage in small talk either, so they didn't. When Freida was finished, Veronica's long brown hair was chin length with bangs . . . and golden blonde.

Luke stepped into the room then.

"What do you think?" Freida asked.

"Perfect. Thank you."

She packed up her things without further acknowledging Veronica, and left.

Luke sat on the leather sofa and watched her for a long time. He'd dressed her today in a corset and jeans. Trish's clothes had been packed away as the new things Luke kept buying slowly replaced them.

"You don't look like her anymore," he said. He handed her a mirror, and it was true. With the bangs and new color, the resemblance had all but disappeared.

He went out into the hallway and came back with a large, wrapped box. "I got you something."

Veronica tugged at the red ribbon, and then tore through the gold wrapping paper. Inside the box, wrapped in tissue, were a pair of cowboy boots in her size."

"I prefer you without shoes, but when you need them, you can wear them. Will you run from me?"

"Where would I go?"

"Good answer, princess."

She put the boots on and went outside. The temperature had started to turn warm again, the first hint of spring easing its way into the air. She lay in the grass, looking up at the sky and the clouds that had turned fluffy again. She stared up at it for a long time, her mind going back to that first night on the road when she'd stopped and stared up in awe at the stars, and then the day of the branding, where she'd fallen asleep watching the clouds blend and merge through the euphoria of the endorphin rush. She'd felt open and free.

Luke joined her a few minutes later and lay beside her. "What are you thinking about?"

"You were right, I love this sky. I love this ranch."

"Thank me for bringing you here," he said. The day he'd told her she'd politely thank him by the time he was finished with her flashed through her mind.

"Thank you, Master."

A tear slid down her cheek, but Luke didn't see it. He seemed preoccupied with pretending he wasn't crazy—as if he could allow her to be a separate person from his tragic love. But the gestures: the hair, the boots . . . they meant nothing. When he'd looked at her, after Freida was finished . . . it hadn't been with the same intensity as before. There had been a note of disappointment that had registered in his eyes for a moment before quickly flitting away.

No, Veronica saw clearly. Soon her roots would grow out, and Luke would let them. She'd be back to the way she'd looked before, as if today had never happened. She'd traded one slavery for another, one lie for another, no more in control of her destiny than before—no matter how much hedonistic pleasure this version brought her. The irony of it all was that she could have been the gold standard, but now she'd stand in the shadow of a ghost, forever clawing for the love and approval that had so easily been given to the other woman.

She blinked back the tears before they could overwhelm her. If he couldn't love her, this had to be enough. The pleasure. The clean air and peace. The freedom from her debt. As she looked up, bright blue with dots of cotton candy clouds filled her vision. In the end, the sky was the only thing that was real.

Other Titles by Kitty Thomas:

Comfort Food
Guilty Pleasures
Tender Mercies
The Last Girl
Submissive Fairy Tales

CPSIA information can be obtained
at www.ICGtesting.com
Printed in the USA
LVHW110042191122
733541LV00015B/347/J

9 781938 639050